STAR HAVEN?

Three days after asking the Captain of the Earth mothership to land his party of technicians and colonists on the planet Hyperon, Commander Williams has every reason to worry. He'd assumed that there'd be records left by the original settlers that would tell him what'd happened to the 500 men and women who'd been dropped here ten years ago to colonize this new world.

But there *aren't* any records—at least any that make sense—and the colonists have completely vanished, abandoning their homes, their equipment, even their household goods! Is the planet itself inimical to human life? The air's always pleasantly warm, there's no animal life to threaten anyone, and the vegetation grows profusely everywhere, and produces a diversity of edible fruits year round.

In every respect, this is a paradise world, a brand new Eden. But if that's the case—*where are the people*?

Borgo Press Books by E. C. TUBB

Enemy of the State: Fantastic Mystery Stories
The Ming Vase and Other Science Fiction Stories
Mirror of the Night and Other Weird Tales
Sands of Destiny: A Novel of the French Foreign Legion
Star Haven: A Science Fiction Tale
Tomorrow: Science Fiction Mystery Tales
The Wager: Science Fiction Mystery Tales
The Wonderful Day: Science Fiction Stories

STAR HAVEN

A SCIENCE FICTION TALE

E. C. TUBB

THE BORGO PRESS

MMXII

STAR HAVEN

FIRST BORGO PRESS EDITION

Published by Wildside Press LLC

www.wildsidebooks.com

DEDICATION

To the Memory of
Authentic Science Fiction Magazine

STAR HAVEN

STAR HAVEN

To Captain Barker, interstellar flight had long lost any thrill it might once have had. It was too much like driving a bus with its predicted stops, regular flights and long months of boring routine between planetfalls. The procedure was always the same. A moment of strain as the ship snapped out of hyper-drive, an indescribable wrenching and a brief nausea as the familiar stars replaced the swirling rainbow patterns on the screens, then the ship would swing into matching orbital velocity with the target planet, contact made, the business done, and they would be on their way again.

He sighed as he leaned back from the control panel, staring idly at the mottled green-brown-blue ball seeming to hang motionless below them, and nodded towards the one man who, technically, had no right at all to be in the control room.

"Well, commander, there she is. Hyperon, second planet of Procyon. A nice new Earth-type world suitable for habitation and exploitation, and your future home."

Williams ignored the elderly captain's remarks, his eyes gleaming as he stared at the glowing screen.

"When do we land?"

"We don't. The ship doesn't, that is. We'll drop you and your people by auxiliary." Barker twisted his head and stared at the radio operator. "Made contact yet?"

"Not yet, sir."

"No?" Barker frowned. "That's odd. Keep trying and let me know immediately they answer."

"Yes, sir."

"They're probably asleep," said Barker, and smiled at the expression on the young man's face. "Don't forget, Williams, it's been ten years since a ship called here last. You can hardly expect them to maintain a continuous radio-watch."

"Why not?" Williams made no attempt to disguise his impatience. "The manual specifically orders that such a watch be maintained. There can be no excuse for failure to comply with the instructions." He frowned at the screen. "Another thing. The settlement was based at the edge of that lake, wasn't it? Where the river runs through that forest?"

"Was it?" Barker stared thoughtfully at the mottled ball. "Could be."

"Don't you know?"

"I could find out," snapped Barker, annoyed at the other's tone. "But if you think I can memorize the exact whereabouts of a hundred different settlements on a hundred different planets then you want to think again. That's what files are for."

"Never mind the files."

Williams reached for the adjustment controls on

the screen. "I've studied up on this planet, and that's where they should be." Abruptly the image expanded, seeming to flow away from the centre as details became clearer, and they stared at the image of a lake edge, a river bank and a tiny, obviously man-made clearing. "There!" Williams rested his finger on the smooth surface. "That clearing, that's where they are."

"Are they?" Barker narrowed his eyes and made a final adjustment, steadying the image against the distortion of atmospheric heat currents. "Looks deserted to me."

Impatiently he glared towards the radioman. "Got them yet?"

"No, sir. The ether's dead; nothing but sun-static."

"Try a flare." Barker looked at the young commander. "Maybe their radio's broken or something. We'll see if any of them attempt visual signalling in answer to our flare." He squinted as a gush of brilliant orange limned the edge of the screen and pointed to a small, spinning shape falling towards the lake. "That should rouse them. Pyrotechnic sound-and-sight attention catcher." He smiled as the spinning shape suddenly expanded into a series of brilliantly coloured smoke clouds, imagining the staccato explosions accompanying the light and smoke.

After ten minutes he said, quietly: "Try another." Then, fifteen minutes after that: "One more and we'll be on our way."

Williams glanced sharply at the elderly captain. "What do you mean?"

"What I said. Unless they answer, we'll get moving. You and your people can return to Earth; it's our next stop anyway, and Hyperon can be written off as a 'bad' planet."

"No."

"Yes." Barker shrugged as he stared at the silent and deserted clearing. "Something's happened down there. Disease perhaps, dangerous native life, something lethal in the atmosphere, any one of a thousand things. It doesn't matter what it is, my orders are plain. Any colony failing to respond to signals is to be considered dangerous and must be abandoned."

"But you can't do that." Williams stared desperately at the screen. "They may be in trouble, or away on an expedition, anything. You just can't abandon five hundred men and women merely because they didn't answer your signal."

"I can and I will," said Barker coldly. He stared shrewdly at the young commander. "I know what's on your mind, Williams. You're thinking that if you return to Earth you'll lose your command. Well, maybe you will, but isn't that better than landing here when you don't know what happened to the others?"

"I can't agree. Earth needs these new worlds, Barker, and too many of them are proving unfit for human habitation. You mentioned a hundred worlds a short while ago. Did you know that, of those hundred, only ten managed to support a colony for the first ten years? You know how things are back home. With the population increase what it is, we've got to find external sources of food and raw materials or face literal starvation. That's why we are founding these colonies. Not for population expansion, though we can use them for that too, but to grow and supply essential food for the home world. You can't just write off this planet because the colony doesn't answer."

"What do you want me to do?" Barker forced himself to remember that the commander was young, impetuous, and with a high personal stake in his decision. "Land and carry a virulent plague back to Earth? You know the dangers of that as well as I do. That is why this ship never lands, but uses the auxiliaries for ship to planet communication. And even if I did land, what then? I've a schedule to maintain and I can't waste time here even if I was equipped for it, which I'm not. This isn't an exploration vessel, Williams; this is only a transport, and, as such, is needed back on Earth for more important things than just worrying about one world." He glanced at the screen and the deserted clearing. "Sorry, but there it is."

"Wait!" Williams swallowed as he looked at the screen. "There's one thing you can do."

"Yes?"

"You can land me and my people."

"Are you crazy?" Barker shook his head and reached for the controls. "You don't know what's down there and you might die within a day." He rested his finger on the alarm button. "No sense in talking about it. You know the rules."

"If you press that button," said Williams coldly, "I'll

have you broken for cowardice."

"You'll what?"

"You heard what I said. You're an old man, Barker, and you've started to think like one. Space isn't for the old, and the Bureau is beginning to realize that. There's a new world down there waiting to be exploited and you've no right to deny my request. If you insist on running from something you don't understand, then I'll see to it that the publicity breaks you."

"You young fool!" Barker surged to his feet, his heavy features mottled with rage. "I'm the captain of this ship and you and every man and woman aboard will do as I say. Damn you! I'll have you thrown in irons for this. Harper!"

"Wait." Williams stepped back as the radioman rose from his seat. "Never mind the rights and wrongs of it. Just imagine what the public will say. A new world, a potential granary, and you ran away from it without even a second thought. And it isn't your skin that I'm asking you to risk. All I ask is that you land me and my people as you were directed to do. What do you think the media will say? The public? They are short of food, Barker, and they pay too much in taxes as it is. Do you think that the Bureau will hesitate to throw you to the lions if it would calm the people? If you think that, Barker, then you're a bigger fool than I thought you were."

"I...." The captain swallowed, his eyes glaring his hate of the young man, but he gestured Harper to return to his chair. "What about the others?"

"My people?" Williams shrugged. "I'll take full responsibility for them. You will land us?"

"You know what you're doing, don't you?" Barker glared his contempt. "I know just what your threats are worth; you aren't concerned with what the people will say and think; all you're worried about is losing your own little world to play the dictator in. To satisfy your own conceit you're willing to risk the lives of fifty innocent people on an unknown, and as far as we can determine, lethal world. I thought that you were low, Williams, but I didn't think that any man could be that selfish."

"That's enough!" Anger glowed in twin spots of red on the commander's cheeks. "I'm not asking for your moral condemnation, and the future will prove that I'm right. Progress is determined by the sacrifice of the individual for the majority, and what does it matter if a thousand die so long as the race is advanced on the path of its destiny? In any case, we won't be as helpless as you seem to imagine. The original colonists had plenty of equipment and we can use that. My people are mostly trained personnel, scientists, the men and women who were to study Hyperon as soon as the economy of the settlement could afford to support them. We'll get along."

"You'll get along, you mean, don't you?" Barker openly sneered as he stared at the young commander. "What do you care for the others?"

"Never mind that. You'll land us?"

"Not so fast." Barker settled himself back in his

chair. He seemed to have lost his anger and looked at the commander with an almost amused contempt. "Don't think that you can bully me, Williams. I don't need a young snippet like you to threaten me with adverse publicity, and don't forget that I happen to have a few more contacts than you imagine. If it came to the point, you would be the one to suffer, not I." He glanced at the screen and the empty, too-small clearing shown on it. "If you land you know that it will be ten years before a ship makes contact?"

"I know."

"And yet you want to be cooped up down there with men and women who will know that you've tricked them as soon as they land."

"I am their commander."

"I see." Barker looked towards the radio-man and shrugged. "All right, Williams. You can have your kingdom—but your people must be warned and given free choice."

"You insist?"

"Yes."

"Then I have no choice. You'll land us?"

"You will also sign and thumb-print a waiver accepting full responsibility?"

"Of course."

"Very well, then." Barker sighed heavily as he stared at the screen. "I'll land you—and I hope that you get just what you deserve."

He didn't look at the commander as he gave the necessary orders.

* * * * * * *

Three days later Williams began to feel the first stirrings of doubt. At first the whole thing had seemed so simple. They would land. From records undoubtedly left by the original settlers they would know what dangers faced them, what had happened to the five hundred men and women set down to colonize a new world, and they would be able to act accordingly. But it hadn't worked out like that.

For one thing there were no records. For another there were no traces of any of the colonists. And suddenly the entire project began to take on a new and more sinister aspect. Not that the planet had shown any animosity towards them; quite the reverse in fact. The air was warm, the sun not too hot, the vegetation profuse and heavily laden with a diversity of fruits. In effect it was a paradise planet—but where were the people?

Irritably, Williams glanced up from his desk as a shadow darkened the papers before him, then nodded as Hermitage dropped into a chair.

"Hello, Doc. Find anything?"

"No."

"Did you examine the huts? The surrounding soil? The...."

"I know my job, Williams," snapped the doctor. "As far as I can see there isn't a trace of the original settlers to be found, but I've made a few deductions."

"Save them." Williams thrust away his papers and eased the collar of his too-tight blouse. "Seen Gerald?"

"He's around. Why?"

"We're having a conference as soon as he gets back. Something must have happened to the colonists and I want to know what. Do I have to tell you why?"

"You do not." The doctor sounded very grim. "Now that the ship has gone we're stuck here, like it or not. If there's some bug lying in wait for us, or some native lurking in the forest waiting to use us as food, then we'd better get ready. Ten years is a long time."

"Regretting it, Hermitage?"

"Perhaps. Maybe it would have been a good idea if this half of the contingent had returned with the rest. Ten women and twenty men aren't really enough to develop a new world."

"But enough to find out just why it hasn't been already done." Williams glanced up as a second man entered the hut and frowned as he noticed the rumpled trousers and lack of uniform blouse. "Improperly dressed, Gerald?"

"Improper, hell! It's crazy to walk about in uniform in this heat. The proper dress for Hyperon is shorts and a coat of suntan—and you could do without the shorts."

"Perhaps, but you will please remember to wear uniform at all times."

Gerald made a rude noise, grinned at the expression on the commander's face, then winked at the doctor as he slumped in the remaining chair. "Shall we get on with it?"

"A moment." Williams stared through the open

doorway. "What are the others doing?"

"As you ordered. Tidying up the settlement, checking stores and equipment, arranging their stuff and setting up laboratories." The ecologist yawned and sagged even deeper in his chair. "Don't talk about work; the very thought of it makes me tired."

"Then you're going to be very tired," promised Williams curtly. He glanced down at his papers. "We've been here three days now and it's time we correlated our information. I've collected every scrap of written material in the settlement; there is surprisingly little of it, and none of it helpful."

"I wouldn't say that," protested Hermitage. "We know the analysis of the air, water and soil. We know the seasonal changes and other astronomical data. We know that nothing harmful to man was found in the first tests, and...."

"Please, doctor." Williams didn't look at Hermitage. "By 'help' I meant of course our main problem. You will naturally retest the water and air and other things you mention."

"Retest? Why?"

"We cannot afford to take anything for granted. The first tests obviously were faulty and it is up to us to discover in just what way."

"I don't see that."

"No? You surprise me, doctor. If everything is well here then where are the people?"

"How do I know?" Irritation swelled the doctor's neck. "I know where they aren't. They aren't dead and buried, that's for sure. There isn't anywhere near that amount of graves in the vicinity."

"There are some though?"

"Yes," admitted Hermitage reluctantly. "About fifty."

"About? Aren't you certain?"

"Fifty-two then, to be precise. All men. I dug them up to make sure. Does that satisfy you?"

"It checks with the official record," said the young commander quietly. "But was it wise to disinter them?"

"The graves were shallow and there was no danger. I merely uncovered the skulls and reburied them immediately after examination. The graves were old and no flesh remained on the bones."

"Marks of fire?" Gerald leaned forward, his eyes serious. "Had the bodies been burned?"

"Yes."

"What?" Williams stared his horror and instinctively moved away from the doctor. Hermitage grunted his contempt.

"No need to get scared. The burning was obviously a precautionary measure and, anyway, they couldn't have died of plague, certainly not any alien infection."

"Why not?" Gerald narrowed his eyes in thought. "You're not going to tell us that old one about alien bacteria not being able to live in a human organism."

"That truism," said Hermitage stiffly, "still applies. Divergent species cannot infect each other with their own peculiar afflictions. Have you ever heard of a man suffering from tobacco mosaic? Or a rattlesnake with mumps? Or a man suffering from hard pad or distemper?

Those illnesses are all native to Earth and yet they remain confined to special groups. What chance then has an alien bacteria to infect a man and find within his body conditions suitable to their growth?" He gestured impatiently as the ecologist started to speak. "Oh, I know all about what happened on Alpha Four, and I'm not saying that it couldn't happen again, but that was a freak, and we're not likely to run into it again."

"Once was enough," said Williams grimly. "That's why the transports refuse to land. If it happened on Alpha Four, why couldn't it happen here also?"

"It didn't," snapped Hermitage; then, as he saw their expressions: "Damn it all, can't you see it yet? Fifty-two men died out of five hundred men and women. All right. But does that make it a plague? Of course it doesn't, and if it was what you're both afraid of, there would be evidence of it. Bodies lying where they had fallen, the huts burned, a litter of dead, but have we found anything like that? You know very well that we haven't. No, you can cut plague right out. I'll stake my reputation on it."

"A very one-sided bet," murmured Gerald, then took the sting from his words by smiling at the irate doctor. "Did you find anything else?"

"No."

"Nothing at all, doctor?" Williams raised his eyebrows.

"I've dug up fifty-two graves since we landed," said Hermitage tightly. "I've been over every inch of the settlement and covered most of the clearing. How much do you expect a man to do in three days?"

"There'll be time to rest after we have found what happened to the others," snapped Williams. "Now is the time to work."

"Oh? Then what have you done?"

"Gerald?" Williams ignored the question. "Did you discover anything important?"

"In three days?" The ecologist shrugged. "I did my best, but it isn't much. The bushes—you can hardly call them trees—seem to bear a continuous supply of fruit. By that I mean that there are flowers, buds, immature and mature fruit all on the same plant. That seems to be general with every plant I've examined. The trees proper, some of them grow over three hundred feet tall, are all nut-bearers. Some have fruit similar to a coconut, others have fruit like a brazil; there are a multitude of types, but all have that one thing in common. They all bear a continuous supply of fruit."

"Isn't that unusual?" Hermitage seemed to have recovered his good humour; at least he had lost his angry flush.

"Very unusual," agreed Gerald. "So unusual that I'm tempted to believe that it is no accident."

"How do you mean?" said Williams sharply. The ecologist shrugged.

"We know that, owing to the almost circular orbit and lack of axial tilting, the climate here is very constant. Even at the poles it never gets cold enough to allow the formation of ice caps, and here at the equator we live in a perpetual summer of even days and nights. That would help account for the lush vegetation, but...."

"No climate would account for one plant bearing both flowers and fruit at the same time," snapped Williams. "The entire concept is against nature."

"Whose nature? Earth's or Hyperon's? They needn't be the same, you know. That's one of the things we've got to find out. And, when you come to think of it, it isn't any more incredible than several types of fruit growing on the same tree. They do it quite often back home. Graft an apple on a pear, several types of apples on the same tree, and even I believe, two or more kinds of soft fruit on the same branch. That's against nature too, but it works. I've seen it."

"Freaks," said Williams irritably. "Distortions produced by the hands of men. Are you trying to tell me that these plants are the product of some alien race?"

"No, not that exactly, but it's something to think about."

"Maybe, but we have no time or concern for idle speculations." Williams riffled his papers. "Anything else?"

"Little insect life. What there is seems mostly to be some sort of bee, and there is a beetle that lives in the dirt and apparently acts like the scavenger beetles back home. No birds, no signs of any animal, just bees to pollinate the flowers and beetles to clear away the debris. A nice neat system."

"Yes." Williams looked down at his desk. "I have here the official record of the original colony. I'm afraid that it doesn't tell us much; for some reason the entries weren't kept regularly. I won't bother with reading it to you; you can read it later if you wish, but it is the only concrete thing we have to go on." He riffled the pages. "Landing, setting up of prefab huts, burning a clearing, assembling the helicopter and power pile." He glanced at Gerald. "The plant is still working, by the way, but there is no sign of the 'copter." He returned to the book. "The first death took place within a month of landing. Red spots, fever, some delirium and great pain. At first they thought it was plague but it didn't appear to be contagious. Other deaths followed all pretty close to each other. Bodies were buried and burned in their graves. All the deaths were those of men." He turned more pages. "Initial crops planted. Apparently they were never harvested, and there is no mention of any large-scale exploration." Irritably he slammed the volume shut and banged it on his desk.

"The first commander must have been a fool. He didn't even bother to keep his records correctly. The entries become briefer and briefer, and finally stop. At no time is there a hint of why they left, where they went to, and what made them go."

"I knew the first commander," said Hermitage slowly. "I wouldn't have called him a fool."

"What else was he?"

"Maybe he just got tired of keeping senseless records?" suggested Gerald. "Seems a waste of time to me; almost as bad as growing crops when the trees and bushes are loaded with food."

"That's the wrong attitude," snapped Williams. "Any colony must be run efficiently, and the entire purpose of this settlement was to exploit the planet and grow food for export to Earth. That is why we are here, and I suggest that you keep our object in mind."

"You said that they left," said Hermitage thoughtfully. "What makes you think that?"

"Isn't it obvious? Are they dead? If so, where are their bodies? Did something come out of the lake and snatch them away? If so, why wasn't it recorded? No, all the evidence points to one fact: that they must have left of their own free will. They deserted! They walked out on all they had done and left their equipment and supplies to rot, and went—where?"

"It's a big planet," said Gerald slowly. "They must have taken the 'copter, of course; that would be the logical thing to do."

"As far as I can remember," said Hermitage dryly, "a helicopter, one of the portable ones, that is, can carry four men at a time. Allow one for piloting, and that leaves four hundred and forty-seven men and women to shift by air. A hundred and forty-nine double journeys. Logical? When they could have walked?"

"Walked to where?" Williams banged his fist down onto the desk. "This discussion isn't getting us anywhere. I must remind you that we have no time for idle speculation; it is essential that we find out what happened to the first settlers. It isn't important to argue about where they went or how. We must find out why! What made them forget their duty to Earth? Why did they neglect their sacred trust? That is what we must discover and, in the meantime, we can continue with the work they neglected to do." He rose to his feet.

"Gerald! You will work with Hermitage and determine whether or not the local fruits are edible and harmless. Hermitage! Despite your conviction that we have nothing to fear from alien disease, I want you to test and test again everything and anything that could menace our health. Ignore the previous records. If they showed their neglect in one thing, they may have been careless on others."

Hermitage nodded and rose to his feet. "Is there anything else?"

"Not at the moment."

"Then I'll get to work. Coming, Gerald?"

"Sure." The ecologist rose and stretched himself. Williams glowered at him then, just as he was about to leave the hut, called after him.

"Gerald!"

"Yes? What is it?"

"Your uniform. Wear it."

"Wear it? But...."

"That's an order, Gerald!"

"I...." The ecologist thinned his lips; then, the habit of a lifetime asserting itself, nodded and stepped into the brilliant sunlight.

Williams smiled as he returned to his desk.

* * * * * * *

The settlement was too quiet. Among huts and sheds

built to hold five hundred, the thirty-one members of the second group were lost. Williams walked from group to group, giving terse orders, watching the slow progress, and always the main question faced him wherever he turned.

Why?

Why had they gone? Where had they gone? Were they all dead, their bodies hidden somewhere on the planet, or were they still alive, captives perhaps, or what? He didn't know, and as the days passed, the conviction grew that he would never find out.

He examined the huts a dozen times, carefully scanning the walls for scribbled words, turning the scanty furniture for a mislaid scrap of paper, a letter, anything to throw a light on the problem, but it was always the same. Nothing. The equipment was in good condition, the workshops ready to be used, and even the farm tractors were still operable once they had been stripped and reassembled. Power flowed from the atomic pile, and the whine of engines echoed over the silent planet as great machines tore at the dirt and seeded the fertile ground with seeds from the bulging stores.

But why hadn't it all been done before?

It annoyed him. All his life he had been used to the obeying and giving of commands, and in his universe there was no room for doubt. Discipline was everything and orders were things to be obeyed blindly and without question. Nothing should have stopped the first colonists from doing their job—nothing, that is, but death, and apparently they hadn't died. He paused by the door of a storeroom, watching a tractor make its slow way across the too-small clearing, then stepped inside the cool dimness. A woman looked up from where she sat sorting seeds, then stared down at her task again.

Williams was used to this. For some reason the others tended to ignore him and, while obeying his orders, made no effort to accept him as a friend, volunteer conversation, or treat him with other than a distant courtesy.

Not that he minded. He was firm in the conviction that a commander should not permit undue familiarity with his subordinates, and his insistence on the wearing of correct uniform had done nothing to make him popular.

"How is it going?" He stepped towards the woman and stared down at the heaps of glistening seeds. "Fertile?"

"Mostly, sir." The 'sir' sounded very stilted. "I'm testing them now for germination."

"Good." He frowned at the bulging sacks. "Have you any idea whether or not these are native produced?"

"They are all terrestrial seeds, sir. They were brought here with the first settlers."

He nodded, waiting for her to elaborate on the bare statement; then, when she did not, sighed and asked the obvious question.

"How long would you say they have been here?"

"About ten years, sir."

"Ten years! But that's impossible! They planted at

least one crop."

"Perhaps they did, sir, but these seeds are ten years old." She stared up at him, her features an expressionless mask, but somehow he had the impression that she was laughing at him. "Could it be that they planted some other crop than wheat?"

"It's possible," he admitted, then frowned as he tried to remember what the records had stated. "I believe that the first planting was one of maize."

"That would account for it, sir. These seeds are those of wheat."

"And they never used them." He nodded and abruptly snapped his fingers. "Of course! If they planted a crop, there should be signs of it. Tell me, would maize continue to grow without attention?"

"If it grew, there should still be signs where it was planted," she admitted. "It would have reverted to a wild state, of course, but it should still be recognisable."

"And yet the clearing shows no signs of cultivation other than bare soil." He stared at the woman. "You're an agronomist, I take it? What's your name?"

"Brenson, Mary Brenson, scientist second class." She rose to her feet. "Shall we go and investigate?"

There were no seeds. There was nothing in the rich black loam but scurrying beetles and normal humus. Williams bit his lips as he watched the girl sift the soil and examine it, running it through her long, slender fingers, finally to admit defeat:

"Nothing, sir."

"And should there be?"

"If they germinated, yes. If not...." She shrugged, wiping her hands on her coverall, and tipped the sample of soil back into its container.

"You mean that they would have rotted away?"

"Perhaps. They could either have shrivelled and remained, or rotted. There is at least one other alternative."

"Radiation?" He shook his head. "The soil was tested for that before the settlers landed. There is no reason to assume that the seeds were killed by an excess of ground radioactivity."

"I wasn't thinking of that," she said slowly. "But did you notice the beetles?"

"You think that they would have destroyed the seeds?" He frowned as he thought about it, acutely aware of the gaps in his knowledge. Commanders were picked for their ability to stick to orders and not for ingenuity and initiative, but even he could see the flaw. "No. If that were the case, how would the native plants survive? If the beetles ate all the seeds, there is no reason why they shouldn't eat roots and other vegetation. Why pick on terrestrial seeds?"

"Some subtle difference perhaps?" Mary sat down as she returned to her task. "If I may suggest a line of investigation?"

"Please do."

"Plant some boxes that have been sifted and freed of beetles. Plant others with beetles. See which grows and which doesn't." Again he had the impression that she was amused by his ignorance.

"Shall I attend to it?"

"Yes." Shyness and a sense of inferiority made him even more curt than normal. "Report to me when you have determined the cause. Give the project top priority." He nodded and walked out into the brilliant sunlight, annoyed with himself for feeling disturbed and yet warm with the satisfaction of getting something done. Gerald waved to him as he crossed towards the hut he was using as an office.

"Commander."

"Yes?"

"I've just finished the tests on the fruit and nuts." Gerald was grinning. "Both edible and harmless and, if I might say so, very nice too."

"You've eaten some?"

"Of course."

"You...." Williams swallowed his anger as he noticed some of the others staring at them with undisguised curiosity. "Come inside."

Within the hut and safe from curious stares he turned savagely on the smiling ecologist. "Gerald, I gave you more credit than to act like an irresponsible fool. How dare you eat the native fruit without my permission?"

"What?" The ecologist blinked then, as he responded to the commander's anger, his mouth set in sullen lines. "Didn't you tell me to determine whether or not the local produce was edible?"

"I did."

"Well?"

"I said nothing about eating it, Gerald, and I also

asked you to determine whether it was both edible and harmless. Do I have to explain to you the difference?"

"Hardly, commander." Anger made the ecologist clench his hands and his voice became brittle with strained politeness. "If I may enquire of the commander, how would he suggest that I determine what he wished to know?"

"Don't act with me, Gerald. You have chemicals, I assume, and techniques by which you can recognize the presence of poisons? Or do I have to teach you your job too?"

"Hardly that, commander, but I would suggest that each keeps to his own. Chemical reagents may be fine for warning us that the fruits contain poison, heavy metals, and other harmful substances, but in the final analysis it is whether or not the human metabolism can assimilate alien food in which we are interested. And there is only one way to do that—eat it and wait. If it can't be digested, it will be rejected. If it can, then, with the aid of radioactive tracers, we can determine whether or not it acts like normal food."

"Interesting," sneered Williams. "So you martyred yourself in direct disobedience to my orders. What do you expect me to do now—give you a medal?"

"No, and I can do without sarcasm as well!" Gerald took a step forward, then remembered who he was and where he was and straightened to attention. "I think that you are being unfair. You gave me a double task, to determine whether or not the native produce was both edible and harmless, and I am perfectly aware of the difference. There could be some unknown element, some combination of vegetable acids or mixture of cellular juices that could prove to be a powerful narcotic, a stimulant, or even a hypnotic. Such things are not rare and, even though some fruits are delectable to eat and perfectly edible, yet to eat them is to become hopelessly dependent on them. The case of the phorypi on Quendis illustrates what I mean. The planet had to be abandoned because of the homicidal frenzy the juices induced. There are other cases, not so dramatic perhaps, but just as insidiously deadly. I cannot as yet tell whether or not the native produce falls into that category, but as there is only one sure way to find out. I acted on the assumption that you would want to know as soon as possible."

"Of course." Williams slumped into a chair, sweating, half-ashamed of his outburst, and yet trying to justify it by telling himself that he was acting for the good of all. He didn't even think of apologizing. To him, that would have been a confession of weakness, and a commander must never be weak. He gestured towards a chair. "Sit down."

"I would prefer to stand, sir, if you have no objection."

"Sit down, Gerald!"

"Yes, sir."

"How long will it take to determine whether or not we can safely eat the native fruits?"

"A couple of weeks, say, a month to make certain."

"I see." Williams stared down at his hands. "Have

you discovered any alternative source of food? Fish perhaps?"

"Not yet. The insect life is rare, but I will test to see whether or not we can eat the beetles. I discount the bees, though there may be honey in the forest. You want me to search the lake for fish?"

"Yes. We can hardly rely on beetles."

"Why not? Many races eat beetles and other insects and a starving man can't be choosey." The ecologist stared at the sweating commander. "Anything wrong?"

"No, but it is as well to be sure about these things." Williams forced himself to sound casual. "After all, we are here for at least ten years, you know."

"I know." Gerald didn't sound too happy about it. "Did you get around to checking the radio?"

"Yes. Nothing wrong there at all and that's another thing that worries me. If the first colonists had discovered something wrong with Hyperon, a disease for example, or an alien menace, or something which made it imperative that they leave the vicinity of the settlement, then why didn't they record an account to be played back to the ship when triggered by the incoming signal? That would have been the simple and obvious thing to do." He sighed. "It's becoming more and more obvious that my predecessor was hopelessly incompetent."

"Hermitage wouldn't agree with you," said Gerald dryly.

"Perhaps not, but Hermitage claims to have known the man. I didn't, and I'm not letting sentiment blind me to the fact that he was criminally negligent in his duties. One thing, however, I can promise. Nothing like it will happen again."

"No?"

"No. From now on a rigorous discipline is to be maintained. No one is to leave the clearing unless they are in parties of five, and all personnel will carry sidearms. I have drafted a schedule of operations and we will hold regular conferences. No one is to leave the clearing at night under any circumstances and, of course, guards will be maintained as at present."

"In other words," said Gerald quietly, "there is to be no relaxation of discipline."

"Exactly."

"Sounds to me as though you expect trouble."

"I expect nothing. I try to anticipate everything."

"And yet in the two weeks we've been here none of us has ever been threatened in any way. There has not been the slightest trace of any animal, certainly none large enough to harm us, and as far as we can determine there is no cause to suspect any danger. Don't you think that your precautions are a little extreme?"

"I am the best judge of that, Gerald. Merely because we have seen no animals doesn't mean that they don't exist."

"I disagree. We are situated on a natural watering place for any large animals and yet we have seen no trace of them. I have ventured into the forest and there are no trails or spoor marks. If there were animals here, they would leave some signs; they couldn't help it, and

I will stake my professional reputation that this area is devoid of animal life."

"I can only quote your own remarks to that asinine statement—it is a one-sided gamble." Williams rose stiffly to his feet. "My orders will be obeyed, Gerald, and it is your duty, as it is that of every man and woman on the planet, to see that they are carried out to the letter. That is all."

"I...."

"That is all, Gerald. You have work to do?"

"Yes—sir!" The ecologist made the title sound almost an insult, and rose to his feet so abruptly that the chair skittered across the floor and fell against the wall. For a long moment the two men stared at each other: Gerald, red-faced with heat and anger, his uniform crumpled and unbuttoned, his hands trembling from the anger boiling within him; Williams, tall and rigid, young and immaculate in his trim uniform, very calm and even a little contemptuous.

"You forget yourself, Gerald. I had intended to ignore your past lapses, but now I see that I have no alternative than to report you for insubordination and lack of co-operation."

"Report and be damned!" Gerald didn't look back as he walked away from the commander.

* * * * * * *

The river was a rippling stream of clear, blue-green water running between high banks and shaded by the tall trees, spilling over a low waterfall as it tumbled down to meet the placid waters of the lake. Gerald lounged against the soft grass, enjoying the feel of sunlight and warm air on his bare skin, and idly watched the bobbing float attached to a crude fishing rod stuck at an angle in the dirt of the bank.

"I think you've got a bite," said Hermitage. The doctor pointed with a stalk of grass and raised himself up on one elbow as the ecologist began to haul in the line. "Another false alarm?"

"Not this time." Gerald grinned as a shiny body broke the surface and wriggled as he swung it through the air towards him. "Look at it!"

"Careful." Hermitage moved away as the strange creature flopped on the grass. "It might be dangerous."

Together they examined the alien fish. It was roughly the same size as a trout, with gaudy colouring and a crest of spines running along the back. The eyes were prominent, the mouth set low on the body, and the fins quivered like the wings of insects as they beat vainly against the air. Suddenly, as they watched, it began to expand, puffing up like a distorted balloon to at least three times its original size and looking a little like a Japanese dragon.

"Defence mechanism," said Gerald, thoughtfully. "That means it probably isn't poisonous." Gently he removed the fish from the hook and threw it back into the water. Immediately it collapsed, shrinking back to its original size, and, with a blur of fins, darted away to the shelter of the far bank. "That's three types we've found so far. The one that had vestigial legs, the one which folded itself into a prickly ball, and the balloon fish." Deftly he re-baited the hook with a piece of nut. "I wonder what we'll find next?"

"You'll find trouble if Williams ever hears that you've thrown them back without examining them."

Hermitage selected a fresh stalk of grass and chewed the end to a pulp. From further down the river, past the waterfall and at the edge of the lake, a burst of laughter echoed among the trees, and the sounds of splashing rose above the soft thunder of the weir. Gerald grinned as he threw back the baited hook and relaxed again against the lush grass.

"The others seem to be enjoying themselves, anyway. I was surprised that our commander permitted them to go swimming." He looked at the doctor. "Do I recognize your cunning hand in this?"

"Perhaps," admitted Hermitage, easily. "I prescribed recreation for reasons of both health and morale, and, as the human body must be kept clean to remain efficient, it seemed a good idea to combine the two by letting half the personnel go swimming." He cocked his head and smiled as he heard the high voices of women mingling with the deeper tones of the men. "Williams didn't seem to like the idea of mixed bathing, but I talked him out of it. Shouldn't be surprised if we don't have a few weddings soon, and the sooner we get sorted out the better."

"Romance by numbers," said Gerald, sarcastically. "Do you think our commander will approve of all his personnel taking time off for honeymoons?"

"Williams isn't so bad, really. It's just that he's never learned to relax."

"Williams," said Gerald, dispassionately, "is a pain in the neck—and you can quote me as having said so."

"Williams," corrected Hermitage, quietly, "is a product of his environment, and we shouldn't blame him for something he can't help."

"Are you defending him now?"

"No, but I can explain him, and perhaps if you knew him better you wouldn't keep irritating him." He smiled at Gerald's expression. "All right then, let's say that you wouldn't let yourself be irritated by him."

"I'd like to kill him and dance on his bones."

"Why?"

"Because I hate his guts, that's why. I don't mind a row. Damn it, I'm human and we can all make mistakes, but Williams gets under my skin. He lives by the rule-book, and he is always right. He's a machine, a thing without emotion, a damn dictator who considers us all his slaves. To hell with him."

"Have you ever thought that perhaps he's already living in his own hell?" Hermitage tipped his stalk of grass into the river and stared at the ecologist. "He's an orphan, you know, and he's never known affection or the warm comfort of family life. As a boy he entered the Academy and lived beneath a spartan regime where discipline was the be-all and end-all of existence. Do this. Do that. Do the other. Obey, and obey, and obey, until it was so drilled into him that he had almost lost his own individuality. He grew up in the belief that to relax was immoral, to find enjoyment other than in work a crime, and his Bible was the rulebook and manual. Now he can't help but follow his indoctrination. You know, of course, that he wanted Captain Barker to land us all here without informing us that the original colony had failed to reply to signals?"

"I know; one of the crewmen told me. Just the sort of thing I would expect from Williams."

"But you can't blame him. Hyperon was his one chance to be something and somebody. He took that chance, and couldn't understand why we would possibly object to obeying orders from a higher authority. He was the commander; we were mere extensions to himself. To him it was as simple as that."

"Didn't he think that we might object to going to our deaths?"

"I doubt if he ever considered it." Hermitage reached for a fresh stalk of grass. "You know, his mentality isn't uncommon. We find it less among our own people, scientists and those in kindred trades, because we've had to learn to think for ourselves, but even with us is surprising how we operate under a tremendous deadweight of tradition and habit. With the masses it is even more so. People just don't think for themselves, and those few who do are still bound by false concepts. Take the food shortage, for example. It isn't anything new and it has been obvious for years, centuries even, that one day the Earth would have more people than it could feed. The logical and sensible thing to do, of course, was to have practised intensive birth control, and some people did. The rest just didn't give a damn, and in that they were supported by their own governments. More people meant bigger armies, bigger armies meant war and conquest, and, nature being what it is, wars inevitably resulted in an increased birthrate. We don't have wars now, and so there is no cutting down of the surplus, so we face starvation instead."

"Interesting, but hardly appropriate to our own circumstances."

"That's where you're wrong. It has everything to do with us. That's why we are here, for one thing. Even though we're ten light years away from home, yet we have brought our traditions with us. Obedience to a superior officer. Obedience to a code with which, logically, we now have no part. Obedience, always obedience, and yet we still never reason out for ourselves why we should obey at all."

"Anarchy?" Gerald shrugged and twitched his rod, more for something to do than for any hope of catching a fish. "We can't have that."

"Why not?"

"Well, it wouldn't work for one thing, and...."

"You see? You mention a word, then refute it in the same breath, and yet you haven't any real reason for refuting it at all. Anarchy, you say, and then immediately state that it wouldn't work—because? You don't know why? You haven't thought about it."

"Well? Would it work?"

"On Earth, no. Our civilization is too interdependent for an individual to exercise free choice. In order to work at all our social system demands that the individual be subordinated to the state. Anyone trying to practice anarchy would soon be crushed by the majority who, while not knowing just why, recognize the fact that their existence depends on total obedience to the dictates of law and order. In such a society no one dares to be too different. You know of the chickens, of course?"

"Yes. Take a chicken, dye it a different colour or make it in some way quite different to a normal bird, and the rest of them will kill it. The herd complex."

"Exactly, and that is just how men live today. Fit in, and you're safe. Be different and you're scorned, jeered at, despised, and in some cases, actually murdered. With thousands of years of that tradition behind us, how can you expect a man to be different from what he is?"

"I don't know." Gerald rose to his feet and, walking up the bank, pulled several lush fruits from a bush. Returning, he handed one to the doctor and immediately bit into one of the others. Juice trickled down his chin and dripped onto his bare chest. He looked at the untasted fruit in the doctor's hand.

"Go on and eat it; it won't hurt you."

"Perhaps not, but you know the orders."

"Orders?" Gerald almost choked as he doubled with laughter. "And you're the one who has been preaching to me about thinking for yourself. Williams says, 'mustn't touch,' and you, like a good boy, obey the nice commander."

"There's a good reason for that order."

"Sure there is. While he controls the rations, he controls the people. I've been eating native produce for a month now and it hasn't harmed me a bit. More than that, I wouldn't eat other food now if I had the choice of any dish on Earth." He finished the fruit, licked his fingers, and reached for another. "Anyway, you'll have to get used to it soon."

"Why? In this climate our own crops should grow pretty fast and we have plenty of stores."

"You mean we found plenty of stores when we arrived," corrected Gerald, evenly. "The more I think of it, the crazier it was to land here as we did. Williams must either have been a supreme optimist or he knew more than he told us."

"Neither. He worked on the assumption that the first colonists would have done all they could to carry out their orders. He hoped to find intact machinery, bulging granaries, planted crops. In short, he expected to find that all the work necessary in taking over a new planet had already been done. It was a reasonable assumption."

"You think so?" Gerald shrugged. "I disagree. We still weren't sure that plague hadn't killed them off, or that the native food contained some subtle poison which could kill after several months. If it wasn't for the absence of bodies we still couldn't be sure, but now we can rule that out; at least I hope that we can. If not, then I'm going to be a very sick ecologist." He didn't seem at all worried.

"Then why did you come if you thought all that?"

"Why?" Gerald looked thoughtful. "I'm not really sure. Adventure perhaps? The desire to pit my wits and skill against an alien environment? Maybe just because I was bored with interstellar flight and wanted to stretch my legs? I don't know. Do you?"

"You came because Hyperon was a challenge and you are a man. Men have always met their challenges; that's why we rule our own planet and are heading towards the stars. I don't think that you need probe your emotions to discover why any of us did what we did.. You're as much a creature of your environment as Williams is of his." Hermitage smiled as he rose to his feet. "Think about it for a while; it may help you to understand him a little better."

"Where are you going?" Gerald finished the last of the fruit and wiped his mouth with a handful of grass.

"Down to join the others. You've eaten, but my stomach warns me that it's time for me to eat, too. Coming?"

"May as well." Gerald lifted his line from the water, frowned at the empty hook, and shook his head as he wrapped the line around the crude rod. "They're getting crafty. Notice how they ate the bait without getting themselves caught?"

"I...." Hermitage stopped, his face blank and seeming to be drained of all life and feeling. Gerald froze, his head tilted as, rising above the murmur of the waterfall, a sound lanced through the soft air.

The sound of a woman screaming in an ecstasy of

terror.

For a moment shock held them rigid, then, with an explosion of smoothly directed effort, they swung into action. Gerald dropped his rod, snatched up his weapon belt, and tore the pistol from its holster as he ran towards the sound. Hermitage followed, crashing through the shrubs and swearing as his foot slipped on the grass. Both men broke onto the shore at the same time and jerked to a halt as they stared towards the lake.

Something threshed on the surface.

It was big, with a smoothly rounded back and a shovel mouth open to reveal a pink gullet. From either side of the wide mouth a long, flat-tipped, tentacle-like appendage extended, the broad, oar-like extremities churning the water to froth as they swept across the lake. Behind it, as if from a hidden tail, spouts of glistening spray shot upwards and made a rainbow pattern against the clear blue of the sky.

The swimmers had all left the water and had run to the far edge of the beach. The men had weapons in their hands, evidently recovered from their clothing, and the women, one of whom still screamed, retreated further toward the shelter of the forest. Even as Gerald watched, one of the men raised his pistol and fired directly towards the great bulk.

The tiny slug couldn't have done much basic harm; in itself it would have been less than a pinprick, but the tremendous velocity with which it travelled was capable of killing a man by hydrostatic shock and even to the sea creature it must have caused pain. Again the man fired, joined now by his companions, and the spiteful snarl of their pistols echoed over the surging waters of the lake.

Red spots showed against the smooth black skin of the rounded back, red spots marked with the white of fat and ruptured tissue, and staring at them, Gerald heard himself yelling a frantic warning.

"Stop it! Cease firing, you fools! You're only angering it!"

He might just as well have shouted to the wind.

The men were frightened. From an ideally peaceful bathe they had been shocked by the sudden appearance of the unexpected and that, together with the nerve-rasping sounds of the screams, had triggered off the only reaction Earthmen knew when faced with danger. *Kill it!*

Kill it so that it can't ever hurt or frighten again. Kill it because it is big, because it is unknown, because it frightened us and we are ashamed of having been frightened. Watching the little flecks of fire from the muzzles of their weapons, Gerald knew that nothing he could do would stop them. Only death would do that. Their death, or the death of the thing that threatened them.

And the thing wasn't dying.

Red foam bubbled about its wounds and waves surged against the shore as the incredible bulk suddenly lunged forward. A tentacle lashed through the air, gouging a wide groove in the sand of the beach and spraying the marksmen with grit. Another surge, and a man, almost doll-like against the thing he faced, went spinning through the air in a twisted mass of broken bone and smashed flesh. The firing halted as they ran from the advancing menace, and Gerald snapped quick instructions as he threw himself forward down the beach.

"Hermitage! They'll be trapped against the cliff unless we can draw it off. Aim for the eyes—if you can see them. Hurry!"

Sand plumed from beneath his feet and the pistol snarled in his hand as he squeezed the trigger, holding it back for continuous fire. Slugs whined towards the glistening bulk before him, and red spots blossomed like ugly flowers as he swung the weapon like a hose, trying to find a vital spot in the huge beast. Beside him, the doctor swore with a dull monotony as he recognized the hopelessness of what they were trying to do.

"It's like sticking pins in an elephant. We're only annoying it."

"I...."

Thunder and a gush of searing flame spurted from the head of the creature, and in the sudden shocked silence following the explosion, they could hear Williams' voice.

"Take cover. All of you get under cover!"

"He's got a projector!" Hermitage dragged at the ecologist's arm. "Let's get away from here. Quick!"

Gerald nodded, and together they ran away from the threshing bulk. As he dropped behind a boulder

Gerald saw Williams, straight and tall in his uniform, standing on the brow of the low cliff, a rocket projector cuddled in his arms. Deliberately the commander took aim and a streak of fire flashed from the muzzle of his weapon to explode in incandescent fury against the head of the sea creature.

It shuddered, writhed, seemed about to lunge forward, then, as if realizing that once fully out of the water it would be utterly helpless, opened its shovel mouth and exposed its pink gullet as if to scream its defiance.

Williams fired directly into the gaping orifice, jerked the loading lever, and sent another rocket projectile after the first before the mouth could close. The twin explosions sounded as one, and with a convulsive shudder, the huge creature relaxed against the sand, half in and half out of the water that was its home.

Even then the commander wasn't satisfied, and not until he had blown off the two tentacles from the thing's head did he lower the projector and descend to the beach. Gerald met him, grinning in relief and admiration at the other's marksmanship.

"Good shooting, commander. Lucky that you used a low-charge projectile at first or we'd all have been deaf or dead by now."

"Call the people together. All of them."

"What?"

"You heard what I said." Williams stared bleakly at the strange monster until the party had assembled. He frowned at the sobbing woman. "What's the matter with you? Are you hurt?"

"No." She took a deep breath and seemed to recover her composure. "I was swimming out in the lake and that thing came up beneath me. I was never so scared in all my life. I screamed and swam back to the others, but it was just like one of those nightmares. You know the one I mean. I just swam as hard as I could but I didn't seem to be able to get away from it. It was as if I wasn't moving at all, and those horrible arms...."

"That will do!" Williams glanced towards the other women. "Take her back to the settlement. All of you. The men will stay where they are." He waited until the near-hysterical girl had been conducted away, then turned to the men. "Who was on guard here?"

They didn't answer. Watching them, Gerald could guess what had happened. The day, as usual, was hot. The water had been tempting and there had seemed little point in two of them standing an unnecessary guard. From the expression on his face it was obvious that Williams had reached the same conclusion.

"Let's put it this way," he said, tightly. "Who was supposed to be on guard? None of you? Or is it that you haven't the guts to own up?" He turned to the doctor. "Will you examine the injured man, please."

"I have." Hermitage didn't move. "I looked at him while you were descending the cliff. He's dead."

"I see. Where were you when this happened?"

"With Gerald. We were catching fish to test for edibility."

"Of course." Williams frowned at the ecologist's

naked torso. "Out of uniform again, Gerald? Or did you have to dive after the fish? Never mind, I'll have something to say to you later. In the meantime will you and the doctor please examine this creature? The rest of you get dressed and carry your dead comrade back to the settlement. I need hardly remind you that, if you had obeyed orders, he would be alive now. I can only hope that you consider your swim to be well worth the loss of a human life."

"That's not fair," protested Gerald. "They...."

"You will obey orders!" snapped Williams, curtly. "I can do without your moralizing. Both you and the doctor will report to me as soon as you have finished. That is all."

"But...."

"Take it easy, Gerald." Hermitage dragged at the ecologist's arm as he made to step after the commander. "What's got into you lately? You two can't meet without a battle."

"The swine! The dressed-up fool! You heard what he said."

"And he was right. I'm blaming nobody, but if they had set guards this wouldn't have happened. Another thing, if Williams hadn't arrived with the projector there would have been more than just one man killed."

"Defending him again? Why don't you go and lick his boots?"

"Why should I? He doesn't like you and you don't like him. Must I hate you because he does? Must I hate him because you don't like him? You're acting like a child, Gerald. A man has the right to pick his own friends and I'm damned if I'm going to share your illogical dislike of the commander just because we are friends. Now, let's get to work."

"Yes." Gerald hesitated a moment, then held out his hand. "Sorry, Doc. I don't know why it is, but I just can't stand uniformed authority. I get a perverse satisfaction out of being deliberately rude, of annoying them, of watching them squirm. They always seem so stupid to me, so illogical, more like machines than men." He shrugged. "I know. If I feel like that then why did join the Service? That's something else I don't know. Maybe I should have my head examined."

"Or your motivations vetted by a psychiatrist?" Hermitage smiled at the other's expression. "When I get time I'll have to straighten you two out, but in the meantime let's get to work."

It was dusk before they had completed their examination of the huge beast, and the combination of hot sun, fish smell, and reeking juices made them glad to leave the hulking shape. Gerald stripped and plunged into the lake to cleanse himself of blood and slime, Hermitage standing watch; then they reversed positions while the doctor washed himself. Then, tiredly, they made their way back to the settlement. Gerald paused at the edge of the clearing.

"Look!" He pointed up towards the stars. "I wonder which one is Earth?"

"Sol, you mean. You couldn't see Earth from here even with a telescope." Hermitage stared up at the night. "I'm no astronomer, but we can find out if you're really interested."

"Should I be?"

"Perhaps—if you're going back there. But if you're not, then why worry? As far as I'm concerned Sol is just another star, and a pretty dim one at that. I...." He let his voice fade to silence and Gerald squirmed beneath the sudden grip on his arm.

"What...."

"Silence." Hermitage pointed towards the edge of the clearing and spoke in little more than a whisper. "See it? Over there beside the seed store?"

"No." Gerald squinted in the darkness. "I can't see anything."

"It's gone now." Hermitage released his grip and spoke in his normal tones. "Probably a trick of light and shade. This dusk and faint starlight is deceptive, but I thought I saw a man standing just by that building."

"What of it? A guard perhaps, or someone out for a last stroll? It could even have been one of the women saying goodnight to her boyfriend."

"Perhaps, but I don't think so. I had a different impression." Hermitage walked slowly towards the dim bulk of the store. "I could be wrong, of course, but maybe we can find something." A small handbeam glowed to life as he pressed the switch, the bright circle of light cutting through the gloom and shining on the soft loam around the building. "Careful now." The doctor moved back and forth, doubled like a monkey, the light shining down towards his feet. It swung, hesitated, swung again, then settled as Hermitage gave a grunt of satisfaction. "There! See it?"

Gerald looked, and swallowed, then looked again, hardly daring to believe what he saw. There, centred in the circle of illumination, stark and unmistakable in the soft black dirt, rested the freshly made imprint of a naked human foot.

The foot of a child.

* * * * * * *

Williams sat at his usual desk, a thick volume open before him and a stylo in his hand. He nodded as they entered, completed his entry in the official record, and closed the book with a grim finality. He seemed tired, his youthful figure had lost much of its vitality, and his eyes reflected the inner turmoil of a man who finds himself up against an unsolvable problem. He smiled as Mary Brenson came from the inner room, a pot of steaming coffee in her hand, then looked at the others.

"Coffee, gentlemen?"

"Thank you, commander," said Hermitage quickly, before Gerald could refuse. "Two cups, please, Mary. It's about time we got this heathen used to civilized habits again." He smiled as he noticed the direction of the commander's gaze. "Commander!"

"Yes?" Williams almost blushed as he looked towards the doctor. "As you can see, Mary here has been invited to the conference. While waiting for you she thought it would be a good idea to brew some coffee."

"Naturally." Hermitage frowned at the expression on Gerald's face. Personally, he thought it a good thing that the commander should find the agronomist pleasant to look upon. There was nothing like marriage for softening up the most stringent martinet, and he was psychologist enough to know that once Williams had enjoyed the warmth of human relationships, he would lose most of his official coldness and protective insistence on inappropriate ritual. "We found something of interest on our way here," he said, casually. "An imprint of a naked human foot beside the seed store."

"A naked foot?"

"That's right."

"Man or woman?"

"Neither. I would say that it was that of a child."

"A child?" Williams stared his incredulity. "Are you certain?"

"Well, no," admitted Hermitage, slowly. "It certainly wasn't big enough for that of a man, but it could have belonged to a small woman."

"Then that accounts for it. It was probably made by one of the women when they returned from the lake. As I remember none of them dressed, and it's possible that the print belongs to one of them." Williams dismissed the discovery and, to Gerald's amazement,, Hermitage didn't press the point. "Now, to get down to important matters. First, did you complete your examination of the beast?"

"We did."

"Would it be possible that such creatures caused the abandonment of the settlement, either by raiding the colony or by making it too dangerous to remain in the vicinity?"

"No." Hermitage sounded very positive. "For one thing, the beast was far too large to have had any manoeuverability outside its natural element. The only thing which it could move out of water were its tentacles, and their range is limited. For another, the gullet was far too small to permit of it preying on any large creature. In this respect it is like the whales on Earth, huge, but able only to swallow tiny life forms, plankton, shrimps, etc. The tentacles seemed to have no other purpose than to sweep water into the mouth. I would say that it was aroused only by the noise and splashing of the swimmers and probably surfaced from sheer curiosity. Also, it mustn't be forgotten that the woman swimmer, even though followed by the beast, was not molested by it, even though it could have overtaken her or killed her with its tentacles. The only thing she suffered was shock induced by fear."

"And yet it killed a man."

"Only when stung by the high velocity pistols. If it had been left alone I believe that it would have returned to deep water."

"Perhaps." Williams stared down at his cup and absently stirred the fragrant liquid. "Mary! Would you like to tell us what you discovered from your test plantings?"

"We'll never grow a natural crop on Hyperon," she

said, evenly. "The seeds will germinate and grow in treated soil, but are eaten by the beetles in untreated media. Obviously we cannot clear the fields of beetles and so we are only wasting time by trying to raise familiar crops."

"Not necessarily," objected Gerald. "The local plants are seed bearing, and that means their seeds must grow. Obviously, then, the seeds must have some subtle chemical, or perhaps a repellant coating which prevents the beetles from eating them. If we could isolate that difference, treat our own seeds with it, wouldn't they grow then?"

"They should, and they probably would, but I have found that it isn't only the seeds which fall prey to the beetles. They will eat the shoots, too. I have raised some short-period crops, cress, mustard, radish, in treated soil and then exposed them to the beetles. They were devoured completely. Your theory about the chemical difference is probably the answer, but it could go further than that. It could be something other than a discoverable chemical. It could be an instinct in the beetles themselves, an odour, a colour even. We don't know and we may never find out. It would take a large-scale laboratory and years of trial and error experimentation to solve the problem."

"So we grow no crops," said Gerald, thoughtfully. "Too bad."

"There is one other way," said Williams. "If we could eliminate the beetles, then we could grow what we liked. Could that be done?"

"Over my dead body."

"Could it be done?"

"I don't know, and I don't want to find out. Altering the ecology of a planet is similar to performing a major operation on a creature you. don't know the first thing about. We've tried it before, remember, and look at what happened. Rabbits were never meant to live in Australia. Some of the early explorers had the bright idea of altering the ecology of the continent by releasing a few pairs and so providing meat for the settlers. Fine—in theory. In practice, as the beasts had no natural enemies there, they increased until they became a menace to the community. So they tried infecting them with a restrictive disease to kill them off, and that worked fine—until the disease spread to countries where there were supposed to be rabbits. It killed them off there, too, and so the foxes and weasels, the stoats and owls, all the creatures who depended on rabbits for food, starved. That upset the ecology still more, and there was all hell to pay until they managed to strike a new balance. Over twelve species of wildlife became extinct through that experiment, Williams, and that was on Earth, a planet we should know something about. What damage do you think we could do if we tried altering the ecology of an unknown world?"

"You haven't answered my question, Gerald. Could you do it?"

"Perhaps. With about a hundred years of experimentation, a full staff and a few shiploads of equipment. Then we'd have some idea of just what we were doing.

Now? As far as I can see there are only the beetles and the bees. You want to get rid of the beetles. So we poison them—if we can, and then find out that they and the bees are in symbiosis and without the beetles the bees die. That means no pollination, no fruits or nuts, no food. Or perhaps the beetles are restraining an earthworm type of culture. End the beetles and the worms eat everything alive on the surface. Is that what you want?"

"You're being insolent, Gerald."

"I'm getting fed up, Williams. You ask a question, I answer it, and then you've got to act all finicky like an old maid getting her stitches right. What's the matter with you? Can't you take 'no' for answer?"

"Cut it out!" Hermitage thrust a cup of coffee into the ecologist's hand. "Drink this and keep quiet." He looked at the commander. "What he says is right. Any attempt to alter the ecology of a planet is asking for trouble. We can either live here or we can't, and if we have to tamper in order to remain, then we shouldn't be here at all."

"I agree," said Mary, quietly. "My recommendations are that we either abandon the idea of growing our own foods or, if we have to, grow them in isolated soil or in hydroponic tanks."

"That's no alternative, Mary." Gerald looked at the coffee as if he hadn't seen it before. "You know as well as I do that to grow food like that would take up all our time and, anyway, we'd never grow enough for export. Personally, I think the whole discussion is a waste of time. Why should we grow crops when the local produce is edible? Think of all the work we'd save ourselves. Who the hell wants to sweat at farming in this climate, anyway?"

"Can we export the local food?"

"I don't know." Gerald didn't look at the commander. "The soft fruits, no. That's a certainty, though we might be able to dry them in the sun and ship them that way. The nuts and other tree fruit, perhaps. It's still going to take a hell of a lot of work though. Our machinery isn't designed to harvest fruits and nuts. It will have to be done by hand, and we still don't know whether or not the fruit will spoil when exposed to free radiations."

"I see." Williams seemed suddenly very old. "So it all boils down to the fact that we've failed. We can't do the very thing we were sent here to do. As far as Earth is concerned this colony is a dead loss."

"I don't see that," protested the girl. "Earth could still ship out some of the surplus population here. Hyperon has plenty of room for expansion."

"No."

"But...?"

"It wouldn't work, Mary," explained Hermitage, quietly. "For one thing the trip takes too long, and the capacity of the starships is too small. No matter how fast they shipped out people it wouldn't make any difference to the population figures back home. The birthrate would take care of that; children would be born faster than adults could be shipped." He sipped at his cooling coffee. "Earth can set up a culture here, in a way that's already been done, but the old dream of using the planets to take care of the surplus has been exploded long ago. Men breed too fast for it ever to work."

"They did it before," she insisted. "What of the pre-space emigrations?"

"Going from one continent to another is a little different from going from one star system to another, and even then your analogy doesn't hold water. In those days there were far fewer people and emigration wasn't the grim necessity that it would be now. The poor emigrated, the unwanted, the young sons who had no hope of inheritance. It wasn't starvation that drove them, but economic pressure. No, Mary, the commander is right. Our job was to grow exportable foods and now it seems we can't do it."

"But we can try." Williams slammed down his empty cup. "First, we will try and eliminate the beetles. At the same time as Gerald is conducting his experiments we shall concentrate on building hydroponic tanks. Fortunately there is plenty of wood on this planet and we have tools and power machines to cut and rip the trees into planks for buildings. We can start with burning a wide clearing, ploughing the soil and running an electric current through the fields. If that doesn't repel the beetles then we'll try something else. Perhaps we could adapt the waste products of the pile to fashion a low-radiation dust that would not harm our seeds, but would kill off the native life. If we fail at that then we can try again. Perhaps we could dust the soil with a six-month dust, kill the native life, plant and harvest a crop, and then re-dust. I'll have to consult with the atomic engineers about it, but in. the meantime we'll concentrate on building the tanks."

"Wait a minute." Gerald carefully set down his untasted coffee and stared at the commander. "Do I get this right? You want to kill the beetles, after all I told you about ruining a planet's ecology. You want to use radi-dust, and you know damn well what that might do to the soil. You want to slash down the trees to build tanks to grow food that we don't really need. Are you insane or just plain stupid?"

"Gerald!"

"Shut up, you uniformed fool! I've stood all I'm going to stand from you and your ridiculous code of blind obedience to outmoded conventions. Know it or not, what you intend doing is to ruin this world. You know that? You're going to kill it just as the rest of your kind killed Earth. Cut down the forests—and let erosion ruin the fields. Spread radi-dust, and make some nice new deserts. Kill the beetles, and set yourself up higher than God and ten million years of selective evolution. Well, I won't let you do it. You hear that, Williams? I won't let you do it!"

"Gerald, you fool!" Hermitage grabbed at the ecologist and slammed him back in his chair. "Calm down, damn you!"

"Let him go." Williams had risen and stood, one hand resting easily on the butt of the pistol in his belt. "It is time this matter was decided once and for all.

Like it or not, Gerald, I am the commander here and you will do as I order. Exactly as I order, do you understand that? I've stood more insolence from you than from any other man, but I tried to make allowances for you, find special justification for your arrogance and contempt of duly elected authority. It is our duty to grow food here. It is our duty to help feed the starving billions of Earth. They are your people, Gerald, yours and mine, and we owe it to them to obey our instructions. Perhaps this planet will be ruined. Perhaps we will fail, no matter what we try, but I don't intend failing until I have made every effort to do what I was selected to do. What if we do ruin the planet? What if we do wreck the ecology? What is that to us? Space is littered with worlds and, if we fail here, it is still no loss."

"You swine!" Gerald struggled against the doctor's grip. "You stinking, selfish, ignorant swine! Touch a single one of those trees and I'll kill you! I swear it!"

"No," said Williams, quietly. "You will not kill me." He looked at the others, Hermitage, still half-sitting, half-leaning against the writhing figure of the ecologist. Mary, standing, pale and silent, against the wall. "You both heard that threat. I, as commander of this settlement, have been threatened with violence by a subordinate. The penalty, as laid down in the manual, is very clear. Punishment up to and including execution, at the discretion of the highest commanding officer. I am he. As we have no facilities for imprisonment here, and as we haven't the men to spare to stand guard, there is only one thing I can do."

"You're not going to shoot him?" Mary stepped forward, her face very pale in the light of the naked bulb. "Not that!"

"I'm sorry, but you are a witness to his threats. In order to survive at all this settlement must be under a rigid discipline."

"It would be murder," she said. "Murder."

"No. Legal execution."

"But there's no need for it. You could evict him, divorce him from the colony, set him to manual labour, anything. But not death. Not that."

"I have no choice."

"But...."

"Stop begging," snapped Gerald. "Can't you see that he's relishing it? Let him kill me if he wants to. He's got a gun and he's dying to use it, and the more you protest, the more damn righteous and self-justified he feels. In a minute he'll say that he doesn't really want to do it. That he has no choice. That I must be made an example of for the common good. You don't stand a chance with his type. He goes by the manual and he's got the entire Service behind him to back him up and accept the responsibility." He made a spitting noise. "The damn hypocrite!"

"There's a man dead out there, Gerald." Williams gestured towards the heavy, humid night. "He died because there were others just like you. Stupid, cocky fools who thought that they knew best. They wouldn't obey orders. They wouldn't accept instructions aimed at their own good. They knew best, and so a man paid for their ignorance with his life. Perhaps your death will serve to shock them into a realization of just who and what they are. They are soldiers, Gerald, just as you are, just as we all are. Soldiers at war. And, if the enemy we fight is nature and space and alien worlds, yet we are still soldiers at war. And in war there can be no room for sentiment, individual judgments and personal preferences. And so you must die. Not because of any personal dislike or hate. But because you represent the one thing we cannot tolerate. You represent anarchy." Williams sighed and seemed to sag a little, not looking at the shocked features of the girl, but keeping his eyes steadily on those of the ecologist.

"You will be executed at dawn under the conditions as laid down in the manual."

"No." Hermitage rose from where he had been restraining the now-quiet ecologist. "He will not be executed at all."

"Indeed?"

"Indeed." The doctor sighed as he looked at the commander. "The girl is right. To kill him would be murder—and you know it."

"I am acting as instructed by the manual," said Williams stiffly. "If you object, no doubt a complaint can be made to the proper quarters."

"Naturally, but as a complaint cannot be made until after the execution, because until there is an execution there is nothing to complain about, it wouldn't do much good. And in any case, you seem to forget that no ship will contact us for another ten years. But never mind that. You will not shoot him because there are specifications laid down to protect him."

"Are there?" Williams smiled, confident of his own knowledge. "Is he insane? Drunk? The victim of hypnosis or post-operation shock? Is he suffering from wounds or battle fatigue? Space fever or radiation sickness? To me he seems perfectly healthy and in his right mind."

"You've left something out," reminded Hermitage quietly. "What about being a victim of drugs?"

"Inapplicable."

"Is it? When for a whole month now he has been eating nothing but alien food. Food, the ultimate effect of which we still do not know. Are you going to shoot a man who is acting as your test animal because of something he cannot help?"

"The food?" Williams looked sharply at the doctor. "You think it poisonous?"

"No. But I am showing you why you cannot execute Gerald and still be at peace with your conscience. The decision, if you kill him, will be yours. The manual is quite clear on the subject, and the specification fits the case perfectly. I can't prevent your shooting him, but don't for one moment think that you are protected by the manual or by authority, Murder him if you like, but be honest enough to admit the murder."

"I see." Strangely, the commander smiled. "You are right. There is no need for him to die. We must assume that he isn't wholly responsible for his actions and report them accordingly."

"Then you're not going to execute him?" Mary stepped forward, her cheeks glowing with relief. Williams half-moved towards her, then remembering his dignity, stiffened into an official attitude.

"No. I must ask the doctor to keep him under observation, of course, and it would be better if he did not mix with the others. Perhaps it would be as well if he retired now, Hermitage?"

"Yes." Hermitage jerked his head at the sullen ecologist.

"Come on, Gerald. Drink your coffee and let's get to bed."

"I don't want it."

"Not after Mary made it especially for you?" Hermitage pushed the cup a little nearer. "You can't insult her like: that drink it down."

"No."

"Drink it!" Hermitage snapped the command, then, as Gerald stared at him, smiled. "I'm tired. Get it down and let's get off to bed."

"I don't know why you're so concerned over it, but if it will make you happy...." He lifted the cup and emptied it in three great swallows. "There! Please may I go now, sir?"

"Of course." Hermitage nodded to the commander, smiled at the girl, and reached out a hand to steady his companion as the ecologist suddenly staggered. "What's the matter?"

"I'm sick," groaned Gerald. "My stomach...." He

lunged for the door and the sounds of his vomiting echoed clearly through the night.

* * * * * *

The soft dirt yielded easily to the sharp blade, and as it was lifted, the tiny bodies of scurrying beetles made a shifting web of colour against the rich blackness.

"There they are," said Gerald, fondly. He threw aside the dirt and prodded at the remains of a buried fruit.

"See? Fifteen minutes and it's almost all gone."

"Is that fast?" Hermitage stooped over the shallow pit and watched as Gerald lifted the fruit and slipped it into a plastic bag.

"Pretty fast. The beetles aren't more than half-an-inch long and the fruit was all of three inches in diameter." He smiled as some of the little insects ran across his hand.

"Bold little devils, aren't they?"

"Won't they bite?"

"They haven't yet, and I've given them plenty of opportunity." He pinched one between thumb and forefinger, holding it gently so as not to crush the delicate chitin, and rose with it in his hand. "See? Two well-developed mandibles with serrated edges. Six legs and four antennae. No wing cases; obviously they are incapable of flight, but surprisingly enough, considering how they live in the darkness, they have well-developed eyes. Egg layers, I assume, though I haven't found a nest yet, and with a remarkable set of instincts."

He dropped the insect and watched it bury itself in the loose soil.

"What makes you think that?"

"I've been studying them. As Williams seems determined to carry out his insane plan I thought I'd better know a bit more about them." He looked at the doctor. "Incidentally, thanks for saving my life. I hope the fact that it's taken a week for me to get around to saying it doesn't lessen my gratitude."

"Forget it." Hermitage reached for a nearby fruit and sank his teeth in the succulent pulp. Hs smiled at Gerald's expression. "I've been eating native produce for a week now—most of us have, but I've kept it from the commander."

"Why? Why eat it, I mean. I can understand your keeping secrets from our dictator."

"I have a theory," said Hermitage, slowly, "and if I'm right, trouble's due to break at any moment now."

"Good." Gerald made no attempt to hide his satisfaction. "What sort of trouble? Mutiny?"

"Perhaps." Hermitage stared thoughtfully at the half-naked ecologist. "If it came to that, whose side would you be on?"

"The other side," said Gerald promptly. "If for no other reason than to stop him wrecking this world."

"He won't spoil Hyperon," promised the doctor with a calm certainty. "But he's got to work it out of his system. I've got high hopes of Mary. I think that girl will be the making of him."

"I'd feel happier if you'd have said 'breaking'. When

I think of the way he was going to have me shot...."

"He didn't want to execute you, Gerald, but according to his lights he had no choice. You saw how pleased he was when I showed him a way out." Hermitage grunted as he sat down. "Williams is a typical example of the military mind, and as such is very easy to predict. To him everything is black and white. An action must be followed by a reaction. He lives by the manual because it is his only guide and he knows that, by following it, he can't get into trouble. You had threatened him before witnesses. Unless he took action he would be at fault. When I showed him that he could still permit you to live and at the same time follow the manual, he was almost childishly grateful. Williams isn't a bad man, Gerald; merely one who hasn't yet learned to think straight. He isn't a bit like Lambert, for example."

"Lambert?"

"The commander of the first colonists. I told you that I knew him."

"That's right, I'd forgotten." Gerald sat down beside the doctor and stared thoughtfully at him. "You know, I've got the impression that there's a lot of things you know and which you haven't explained. That footprint for instance. You know as well as I do that no woman ever made that print."

"Of course."

"And it didn't surprise you?"

"Why should it? Even you should be able to deduce who made it and why."

"Who?" Gerald frowned. "There's no one here but

us, unless...." He stared at the doctor. "The first settlers! Is that it?"

"What else?"

"You've seen them, then? You know where they are?"

"I haven't seen them, but I know where they are. They're in the only place they could be. Here, on Hyperon, where they've been all the time." He smiled at the startled expression on the ecologist's face. "Isn't it obvious? They didn't die or we should have found their bodies, and if they didn't die at the settlement, then why should they have died after they left? As for the footprint, when you have almost five hundred men and women, children are to be expected. I imagine that there must be quite a few children by now. Wouldn't it be logical for one of them to have crept near the settlement, driven by curiosity, perhaps, or just from a desire to see if he could find any new playmates?"

"But if they're here, why haven't we seen them? Why didn't they answer the radio call from the ship?"

"Perhaps they didn't want to be disturbed."

"No." Gerald shook his head. "No, that isn't logical. After ten years they would have been glad to hear another human voice, learn the news, catch up with events. They would have answered if only to obtain more tools, supplies, things they must need. It just isn't natural that they deliberately hid from the contact vessel."

"You think not?" Hermitage shrugged. "I'm a doctor, Gerald, and in order to heal bodies I've had to learn a little about the workings of the mind. Nothing men do is ever illogical—to them. No matter how insane a man is, this actions and processes will always be logical—to him. Sometimes I wonder whether or not we haven't reversed the meanings of the words 'sane' and 'insane'. For, when you come to think about it, could anything be more illogical than our own civilization? I told you that I knew Lambert. He was one of the few men I've ever found cause to admire. He managed to remain an individualist in a society that actively discourages individuality. A reader of poems and old books, an idealist, a dreamer if you like. I found him a fascinating study m psychology, and we spent many hours together discussing everything from philosophy to cybernetics."

"Interesting," said Gerald, absently, "but what has that to do with us?"

"Maybe more than you think." Hermitage raised himself on one elbow and stared at the ecologist. "Knowing the man enabled me to know what he would do under a given set of circumstances. He arrived here ten years ago with five hundred men and women, and certain. specific orders. He couldn't carry out those orders, we know why, and so would feel himself relieved of the obligation to do his original task. What would he do then? What would you do?"

"I'm not sure," said Gerald, thoughtfully. "Not as Williams hopes to do, that's for certain." He shrugged. "There's not much you could do when you come to think of it. Explore, I suppose. Do some scientific investigation. As for the rest, well, take things easy, enjoy yourself, kill time until the ship came to take you off."

"Imagine yourself in that position, Gerald. You are in command of five hundred people, who all their lives have never known anything but work. Hard work. Relentless. With no time for leisure or creative enterprise. All their lives they have been bounded by the iron walls of convention and tradition. They owned nothing and never would own even the dirt they would be buried in. They worked in order to live and they could never hope for anything else. Then they come here, still prepared and expecting to work, ready and willing to turn themselves into high-production farmers. Then they find they can't do it. Then they find that, for the first time in their lives, they can eat and sleep, walk and play, without the spectre of poverty or imprisonment hovering over them. They would have time to waste, time to burn, time to do whatever they wanted to do within their limits. What would you do if you were in command?"

"I'm beginning to see what you mean," said Gerald, thoughtfully. "It's a lot of people and you just couldn't stop them if they wanted to go. Anyway, there'd be no point in preventing them once the original plan had flopped."

He looked at Hermitage. "But that doesn't explain why the didn't answer the contact ship."

"I think it does." The doctor gestured towards the fruit-laden bushes and the nut-heavy trees. "Look at it. Food for the mere effort of reaching out for it. A climate that makes the wearing of clothes a ludicrous anachronism. No hostile animals. No harsh seasons. No necessity even to build houses. What would you call it?"

"Paradise."

"Yes. Here men can walk without fear. Here, for the first time in their lives, they could experience freedom, true freedom, not the conditioned meanings usually given to the word. They would have an entire planet to wander in, and there could be no wars, no enemies, no dislikes. If a man offended you, then you could walk away from him. There would be no need ever to see another human face unless you so wished. Freedom, Gerald. Pure, perfect freedom, and once experienced, do you think that anyone would ever relinquish it of his own free will?"

"Anarchism," said the ecologist, slowly. "Decadence. A returning to the primitive and a falling into savagery."

"What makes you think that?"

"What else could it be? We're civilized only because we work at it. Men are basically animals, Hermitage, you know that. Take away their barriers and down they go."

"Down?" The doctor shrugged. "Or up? Is it bad to wander the fields and feel the warm sun and the soft air against your naked skin? Is it bad to feast in convivial company, get drunk, even, sing songs and rid yourself of the pressing urgency to be up and doing? And doing what? Making money? Why, when you could have everything for the effort of taking it? For all a man really needs is food and shelter; supply those and then he can give full rein to his creative instincts. No, Gerald, they wouldn't have sunk into degenerate savages. For they were civilized to begin with. They have a language, which, in itself, is one of the finest tools ever produced. They have intelligence and the keenly inquisitive minds of the intelligent. At first, perhaps, they would have yielded to the lotus, but then, after the novelty had died, they would be itching to do things with their hands again. But this time they would do as they wished and not as they were ordered. Art, carving, the manipulative sciences. They had doctors and technicians; and men love to teach what they know. And there would be children, lots of children, and is there any greater enjoyment than watching your young grow?"

"I wouldn't know, I've never had any." Gerald stared at the surrounding trees. "So you've known all the time what must have happened."

"Not all the time, no, but now I am sure."

"What made you sure? I've been with you all the time and I haven't seen anything. In any case the whole thing is pure surmise. What about the records?"

"Would any commander make such scanty notations? I think we'll find that the original records were destroyed and the book we found deliberately left to misguide. After all, what does it tell us? Some men died. Merely that and nothing more. Not a word about the inability to grow crops. Nothing about the edibility of the native produce. Not even a hint as to why they went. If records were made, they must have been far more comprehensive than that."

"A joke?" Gerald looked his disgust. "A hell of a way to have fun. Anyway, what made you so sure?"

"You did."

"I did?" The ecologist sat up and stared at the doctor. "What did I do?"

"You were sick," said Hermitage, seriously, then rose as a man came crashing through the bushes towards them.

"Doctor?"

"Here."

"The commander wants you to return at once. There's trouble, bad trouble." The man wiped sweat from his face and his eyes reflected his fear. "Hurry."

"Illness?" Hermitage rose quickly to his feet. "Is it sickness?"

"Yes. Hurry!"

* * * * * * *

The man was dying. Hermitage could see that at a glance without the necessity of making a closer examination, but he made it just the same, carefully touching the angry red blotches and pursing his lips at the colouration of the eyes. Williams stood beside him, his attention to duty overriding his instinctive fear of plague, and gestured the doctor outside after the examination.

"Will he live?"

"No."

"Is it catching?"

"I don't think so. How did it happen?"

"That's the mysterious thing about it. He was all right this morning, but just after lunch he collapsed. Those red patches seemed to appear within seconds." Williams swallowed. "Is it plague?"

"No."

"What is it then? Don't just keep saying 'no'. What do you advise?"

"Lift your restriction on the eating of native produce. Serve it at the next meal and see that every man and woman has a fair share."

"What!" Anger thinned the commander's lips. "Must I remind you that this is hardly the time for joking? There's a man dying in there and there may be others. For all you know the native food may be to blame, and yet you ask me to order everyone to eat it."

"I'm not joking, Williams. There's a good reason for my suggestions, and as for the food being dangerous, that's nonsense. Gerald has eaten nothing else for weeks now, and I've lived on it for a week myself. It isn't the fruit which is causing the illness, it is lack of it."

"How do you mean?"

"You don't know much about ecology, do you, commander? It goes a little deeper than just the balance between flora and fauna. It applies to everything on the planet and you can't ignore it. For a long time now we've known that, to remain healthy, a man must eat the food of the region he is in. The old travellers knew that. Explorers ate seal meat and blubber as far as their stomachs could stand it while venturing to the poles. Others made a point of changing their drinking habits to conform to the local customs. Canned food brought a flock of stomach upsets in its wake, not because it was canned so much as because it was foreign. Don't misunderstand me, commander. I'm not suggesting that men died because they ate tinned beef instead of the local food, but I am saying that they were not perfectly healthy. Not that it mattered then; few people really were, and the human body is pretty tough anyway. But now we are on a new world. If it was desirable to eat varying foods on our own planet, how much more desirable must it be to eat local food in differing star systems?"

"If I do as you suggest, will that save them?"

"No, but it will prevent others from dying the same way." Hermitage shrugged. "Some will die, of course. Not everyone can adapt to a new world, but we know that the first colonists managed to halt their deaths and we know, too, that terrestrial food is unacceptable to a metabolism which has become accustomed to native produce."

"So?" Williams looked his disbelief. "How do we know that?"

"Gerald was sick after drinking coffee. I made him swallow it because I was curious to see if my theory was correct. It was. His stomach rejected the caffeine and it made him ill. The assumption is, then, we can eat the fruits and nuts without harm, but to continue with our own food is to clash with the ecology." He shrugged. "In any case we have no choice. The sooner we all become acclimatized the better."

"I don't see that. We have plenty of food and can easily last out ten years on rations. If what you say is true, then that means that if we eat the fruits we won't be able to revert back to a normal diet. I don't feel justified in giving the order which, in effect, would doom all these people to exile."

"Exile?" Hermitage smiled. "Is that what you call it?" He became serious. "We could revert back to our accustomed diet if we had to, but why should we? Contact won't be made again for ten years, and, when they receive no answer, they will write off Hyperon as a 'bad' planet. I...."

"Wait a minute!" Williams' fingers dug into the doctor's arm with a grip which made the older man wince. "What do you mean, 'when they receive no answer'? Why shouldn't they?"

"Did we?" Hermitage jerked his arm free and stared at the commander. "Do you think that we are going to be different from the first colonists? Do you honestly believe that these people are going to be content to wait here for ten years without wanting to eat the native produce? Ten years, Williams. That's a long time."

"I have planned for it. The tanks, the experiments; we shall have plenty to keep us busy."

"And for what? To grow food we can't even eat? To build tanks? Hydroponic tanks when the soil is as

fertile as we could wish? Is that what you call constructive effort?" Hermitage shook his head. "No, Williams.
You know that you'll never be able to retain control
over the colonists that long. Discipline is slackening
already, and how long do you think you can make them
work at useless tasks? If they had a constructive job to
do, things would be different, but you're making work
and they know it. They'll obey you for a while; the dead
weight of tradition, the sheer inertia of the past years
will see to that, and then they'll begin to question, to
dodge, to disobey. One day you'll give a command and
it will be ignored. Then you will have to enforce it or
lose your position. You might be lucky the first time.
You might be able to threaten them into obedience, but
there'll be a second episode, a third, and then, one day,
you'll find yourself alone." He smiled at the serious
face of the young man. "Forget it, Williams. There's
nothing you can do to stop it."

"I refuse to desert, and I refuse to let any of my
command desert." Unconsciously his hand fell to his
holstered weapon. "I have the law to back me up."

"You have nothing but the gun at your belt and the
courage to use it or not, as you decide fit. But one thing
I'll promise you: of you ever decide to use it, then keep
on using it, because if you don't, then you'll be the next
to die."

"Shoot *me*? Their commander?" Shocked horror was
in Williams' voice, and Hermitage could understand
his incredulity. Men just didn't mutiny. Officers just
weren't shot. Men just didn't refuse to obey. Hermitage

rested his hand on the young man's shoulder.

"Look, son," he said, quietly. "I'm a little older than you in years, and a damn sight more in experience. I know that this is hard for you to take, but look at it sensibly. Gerald should have warned you what to expect. He hates you, not as a man, but for what you represent. He doesn't know that himself as yet, but he will. I'll make sure that he does. He hates you because you represent the very thing he's been trying to escape all his life. He hates you because, to him, you are the overcrowded cities, the poverty, the worry, the jobs he doesn't want to do, and the nastiness he wants to avoid. You are civilization. You are the enemy."

"Nonsense!"

"Is it? Why do you think men leave home? It isn't to open new frontiers but to escape from what they hate. That's what we're doing, all of us. That's why we volunteered for space; not to spread the culture of man but to get away from the insane rat race back home. All of us carry that dream, and all of us hope that, some-where, someday, we shall find paradise." He gestured towards the sky, the forest, the tall shapes of the trees. "And here we have found it. Here, on Hyperon, we have found the very thing for which men have been searching from the beginning of time. A place to rest. A place of warm comfort and relaxation. And, now that we've found it, do you think that we could ever give it up?"

"I don't believe it," said Williams, slowly, and yet deep within him something admitted the truth of what Hermitage had said. He had volunteered for the Academy to escape the harshness of the orphanage. He had volunteered for space to get away from the sneers of his fellow officers, the unspoken gibes and cold indifference of those to whom he was an outcast.

And he had even volunteered to land on Hyperon against all sense and logic, to escape being sent back home to Earth. And now?

"What of the sick?" he said, quietly. "The others?"

"I'll take care of them."

"And Earth?"

"Forget Earth. Hyperon is our world now. This is the haven we have subconsciously craved all our lives, and now that we've found it, we can never leave. It's ours, Williams. All ours for us and our children. Earth is a bad dream, a thing of the past, a nightmare we can all forget. This is paradise and here we stay."

"Perhaps." Williams drew a deep breath of the scented air, and Hermitage smiled as he stared at the perplexed face of the young commander.

"Don't worry about it now; you'll understand soon enough, but here's some free advice. Forget that you're the commander and set about making some friends. Know what I mean?"

"I think so." Williams smiled as he stepped forward to where a woman waited with the age-old understanding of her sex and smiled down into her eyes. "Hello, Mary."

"Hello, Bill."

It was all, but it was enough. Williams felt an unfamiliar comfort as he walked across the clearing, the girl at his side. Later he would have to think about altering the records, uncouple the emergency radio tape, and dampen the pile, but there was plenty of time for that.

Now he was eager to explore paradise.

ABOUT THE AUTHOR

English writer **E. C. TUBB** is internationally known, having been translated into more than a dozen languages. In a sixty-year writing career he published over 120 novels, and more than 200 science fiction short stories in such magazines as *Astounding/Analog, Authentic, Fantasy Adventures, Galaxy, Nebula, New Worlds, Science Fantasy*, and *Vision of Tomorrow*.

Tubb's early science fiction novels were exciting adventure stories, written in the prevailing fashion of the early 1950s. Yet, from his very first novel, his work was characterized at all times by a sense of plausibility, logic, and human insight. These qualities were even more evident in his short stories, which were frequently anthologized.

By 1956 his output included adventure, detective stories, and westerns, but he remained best known for his numerous science fiction novels, of which *Alien Dust* (1955) and *The Space Born* (1956) were acknowledged classics. Tubb became famous for his long-running "Dumarest of Terra" series of novels, the galaxy-spanning saga of Earl Dumarest and his search to find his way back across the stars to the legendary lost planet where he was born—Earth. They eventually spanned thirty-three titles, the final one, *Child of Earth*, appearing in November 2008. Equally well known were his *Space 1999* TV novelizations, and his "Cap Kennedy" novels. Some of his finest SF short stories were collected in *The Best Science Fiction of E. C. Tubb* (Wildside, 2003). Tubb continued to write dynamic science fiction novels right up to his death in October, 2010.

THE TIME TRAP

There are six people in millionaire Nick Clayton's chauffeur-driven limousine when it leaves a country house party on its return trip to London: Clayton himself; his girlfriend, Bernice Forbes; Horace Dawlish, his imperturbable servant and driver; the unhappily married financier Harvey Brand and his wife, Lucy Brand; and the tragic socialite, Betty Danvers.

But neither the automobile nor its six occupants ever reach London. Instead, the car drives some thirty miles down a country road—and just vanishes! And when the travelers suddenly find themselves in an alternate reality where time stands still, they begin wondering if they will ever escape...THE TIME TRAP!

Borgo Press Books by JOHN RUSSELL FEARN

1,000-Year Voyage: A Science Fiction Novel
Black Maria, M.A.: A Classic Crime Novel
The Crimson Rambler: A Crime Novel
Don't Touch Me: A Crime Novel
Dynasty of the Small: Classic Science Fiction Stories
The Empty Coffins: A Mystery of Horror
The Fourth Door: A Mystery Novel
From Afar: A Science Fiction Mystery
The G-Bomb: A Science Fiction Novel
Here and Now: A Science Fiction Novel
Into the Unknown: A Science Fiction Tale
The Man from Hell: Classic Science Fiction Stories
The Man Who Was Not: A Crime Novel
One Way Out: A Crime Novel (with Philip Harbottle)
Pattern of Murder: A Classic Crime Novel
Reflected Glory: A Dr. Castle Classic Crime Novel
Robbery Without Violence: Two Science Fiction Crime Stories
Shattering Glass: A Crime Novel
The Silvered Cage: A Scientific Murder Mystery
Slaves of Ijax: A Science Fiction Novel
The Space Warp: A Science Fiction Novel
The Time Trap: A Science Fiction Novel
Vision Sinister: A Scientific Detective Thriller
What Happened to Hammond? A Scientific Mystery
Within That Room!: A Classic Crime Novel

THE TIME TRAP

A SCIENCE FICTION NOVEL

JOHN RUSSELL FEARN

THE BORGO PRESS

MMXII

THE TIME TRAP

FIRST BORGO PRESS EDITION

Published by Wildside Press LLC

www.wildsidebooks.com

DEDICATION

For John Lawrence

CONTENTS

CHAPTER ONE
UNFINISHED JOURNEY

The sound of revelry drifted into the mellow summer darkness on this June evening. The French windows of the great residence were open to the faultless lawns; shadows chased each other in the gloom. Festoons of Chinese lanterns glowed like fireflies and made the solitude of the romantic far too bright for their liking. The music of a dance orchestra, the clink of glasses, the buzz of voices, the laughter of guests.

Henry T. Mythorn was doing things properly, as he had done throughout his life. The millionaire industrialist was in the midst of a house-warming. Mythorn Towers was one of the few ancestral homes left in Britain and Henry T. had seen to it that it had become his. Now, after a year of renovation and improvement, he and his family had moved in—and gathered about them all the guests, friends, and intimates they could find.

Most of them were prepared to stay until the small hours, but not so Nick Clayton. He owned a London cabaret that opened at one in the morning, and he always made a point of being there, no matter what. And

because Nick Clayton was worth several millions—earned by his father before him—he usually had his way.

Outside in the driveway stood his car. Beside it, utterly impersonal, his chauffeur-manservant Dawlish was waiting in rocklike calm. The car was a big, open one and capable of carrying five more passengers besides the driver. The four others who were congregated around Nick Clayton in the hall were ready for departure, though by no means anxious to go.

In fact, Bernice Forbes, Nick's particular girl, friend—at the moment—openly said so. She looked rather like a big doll in her costly fur coat, her flawlessly made-up face slightly pinker than usual with annoyance.

"Can't your manager look after the Club for once, Nick?" she demanded. "Things here are just beginning to warm up."

Nick smiled. It was the smile of a rogue yet with generosity in it. He lived well and heartily and wanted everybody else to do the same. Blond-haired and passably good-looking, he was a playboy who, nevertheless, turned some of his huge financial backings into worthwhile propositions. And the Apex Night Spot was one of them.

"We're going back, Berny," he replied firmly. "I like to handle everything for myself."

Bernice pouted and gave a shrug. Henry T. and his wife, both of them big and opulent, looked disappointed.

"If that is how it has to be, all right," Henry T. smiled, shaking hands. "I don't suppose the rest of us will disperse until the small hours. Pity you can't stay."

"He could if he wanted," commented forty-year-old Harley Brand acidly.

"You said you'd be glad of a night's rest for once," Nick reminded him dryly, and Harley Brand scowled.

He was a financier in the city, heading for wealth too if certain plans matured. His wife, a pale woman of thirty-two, stood beside him without saying a word. In his climb to power the still young Harley Brand had forgotten one thing—to remember how much he owed to Lucy Brand's long suffering patience.

"Well, let's go!" Nick ordered cheerfully. "Just on midnight. We can make it in thirty minutes. Come on, Berny!"

He caught the girl's fur-coated arm and she hurried beside him down the broad steps to where the huge land cruiser with its chromium-plated fittings was standing. Dawlish, the chauffeur, was so immovable he looked like part of the car. He swung open the gleaming doors as the party arrived.

"Hey, wait for me!"

Nick paused and turned as he was about to follow Bernice into the wide front seat. A girl in a light dust-coat, her red hair streaming in the warm night wind, came hurrying down the steps, breathing uncommonly hard for such slight exertion.

"Give me a lift to London, Nick?" she asked brightly.

"Sure thing, Betty. Squeeze in the back."

"Okay. I'm not up to house-warming tonight. My ticker's acting queerly."

Harley Brand and his wife moved up a little to make room for the girl and she settled down beside them and smiled rather woodenly. They smiled back but did not speak. Betty Danvers was a problem girl, and only she knew why. She was twenty-five years of age, pretty, and spent her life in a whirlwind of pleasures and extravagance, drawing constantly on her father's seemingly endless bank account. Some said she was worthless; others liked her brightness.

The chauffeur moved with stiff-necked dignity to the wheel, started up the engine, and then set the huge car gliding down the driveway and out into the lane which ran across country to the main London-south coast road. The wind sweeping past the car was nearly sub-tropical and the stars were gleaming in masked beauty through a high screen of mist.

Presently the car entered Little Brook village with its solitary new signpost saying very definitely—TO MYTHORN TOWERS. Trust Henry T. to think of that! The villagers had apparently retired and the car's headlights swept across scrupulously whitewashed walls and then upon the ivy-clad bulk of the village church. The clock was just striking midnight.

"Ten—eleven—" Nick intoned, then at the twelfth stroke he frowned a little. Instead of booming out it seemed to cut itself off short, like a gong in a radio program suddenly switched out.

"Sounded queer," Bernice agreed, seeing his puzzled

glance. "Probably the bell's as cracked as the village inhabitants."

"Could be," Nick admitted.

By this time the car was on the cross-country road that connected eventually with the main London-south coast major highway. Dawlish sat immovable at the wheel, his cadaverous face lighted by stars and dashboard reflections. The dark field on either side made a perfect background for his profile.

On, and still on, the engine making hardly any sound and the speedometer registering 66 mph. On and on, until Nick began to frown a little as he saw no sign of the broad, deserted road ending. The headlamp beams pierced the misty night for a tremendous distance, but there was only the road, dusty and not very well surfaced, and the great deserted expanses of fields on either side.

"How much further?" Bernice asked at last, sitting up in some surprise. "Dawlish, are you sure you're on the right road?"

"Certain, miss. I turned left at the signpost which brought us on the road along which we came from London."

As if to satisfy himself that the road must end somewhere Dawlish increased speed—up to seventy, and then eighty, but the headlights continued to blaze along a white ribbon which stretched on, on, and ever on until it lost itself in the starry backdrop.

"Stop!" Nick commanded at last, his voice taut. Dawlish obeyed and as the car came to a standstill

there was an appalling quiet.

"What—what's happened?" Bernice asked at last, and she could not be blamed for sounding frightened. "Are we on the wrong road, or something?"

"Evidently we must be, Miss," Dawlish answered. "I set the trip-milometer before we started and we've traveled thirty miles. Yet we're still on this country road."

"I imagine the explanation is fairly simple," Harley Brand said, though he did not sound convincing. "We've hit one of those confounded country roads which go in a circle. If we go on far enough we'll come back to the signpost."

Silence. Dawlish looked at the stars. Bernice, being next to him, was attracted by his action and looked also. And her none too agile brain was puzzled by what she saw.

There was something queer about those stars. Instead of being bright points of light, they were silvery-looking streaks, broad at the top and narrow at the base, as though they had been driven into a great pool of dark and been shorn off in the doing.

Stars like shaved-off rods? Utter silence? The empty fields and nowhere a sign of life or the solitary gleam of a distant lighted window.

"Where the hell are we?" Nick demanded at last, and his enquiry brought them all into action again. They moved vaguely with no fixed idea in mind.

"Circular road, Nick," Harley Brand insisted.

"It's something more than that, sir," Dawlish

responded, a queer note in his voice. "Take a look at the stars. Not only do they look odd, but not one of them has any recognizable position. I've just been studying them."

"I wouldn't know a star from a planet, and even less their positions," Nick growled. "Surprises me you know so much."

"I've studied astronomy, sir, amongst other things. Usually I can find any particular star or constellation, but not this time! And when the stars fail you for direction you're—lost!"

"Ridiculous!" Nick declared, scrambling out of the car. "There'll be bound to be a patrol man along soon, or a passing car, or—or—something."

Nobody answered.

"There'll have to be!" Nick insisted.

"How much petrol have we?" Betty Danvers asked, and Dawlish glanced at the fuel gauge.

"Practically empty, Miss Danvers. I was intending to fill up at the garage just beyond Mythorn—only we haven't passed it."

Again the mystified quiet. Then Bernice exclaimed, "I've got it! Let's look at a road map."

Dawlish dug it out of the cubbyhole and six anxious faces bent over it in the dim glow from the dash.

"Here's Little Brook," Harley Brand said, pointing. "Here is the road leading through it to Mythorn Towers—yes, and here's the spot where the new sign-post has been erected where we turn the corner. Then we go straight to—"

There was no road marked where they had been traveling. They looked at each other with half-closed eyes, striving to mask a deepening apprehension.

"Maybe the map's old?" Betty suggested.

"Recent issue," Nick replied; then, his brows knitted, he looked around him in the quiet. Finally he took a torch from the car's side pocket and flashed the beam at his feet. The road was not macadam-surfaced, but hard-baked soil, not unlike a trail out west which has been subjected to ceaseless sun-blistering. Dust lay thick upon it. It even looked as if rain had not descended for ages—and this, for England, was incredible, dry though the summer had been.

"I don't get it!" Nick confessed at last, and switched off the torch.

Dawlish clambered out of the car and surveyed.

"Maybe we're dead?" Betty Danvers suggested dryly.

"Which isn't funny!" Bernice flared at her.

"All right, girls, keep your tempers," Nick reproved them, sensing the thin edge of hysteria. "We'll work out something—I hope."

He turned and headed round the front of the car to speak to Dawlish, then he stopped halfway, completely astounded. As if things were not bad enough already there was a new mystery added. For, though he was directly intercepting the beam of the offside head-lamp, he was not casting a shadow! The beam tunneled straight on into the dreary emptiness.

Nick glanced back at the car. The girls and Harley

Brand were arguing amongst themselves and had not noticed this latest phenomenon—but Dawlish had. There was a rather grim smile on his lean features as Nick came to his side.

"You noticed that?" Nick asked.

"Yes, sir. Unusual—but explanatory."

"Explanatory? How d'you mean?"

Dawlish lowered his voice. "I don't wish to scare the ladies, sir, so maybe I'd better make things clear to you to begin with. And maybe Mr. Brand, he being the other man in the party."

Nick shrugged and then called, "Hey, Harley! A moment!" Harley extricated himself from amidst the three talkative women and came over to where Dawlish and Nick were standing.

"Dawlish has a theory," Nick said. "Maybe we should listen."

"I believe," Dawlish said quietly, "that we have driven out of our normal space and time into hyper-space."

Nick and Harley exchanged looks.

"Sounds crazy," Harley decided.

"No more crazy than there being no shadows, sir."

Harley started. "No what?"

Nick demonstrated by putting himself in the way of a headlight beam. Unfortunately Betty Danvers witnessed it.

"Look!" she cried hoarsely. "Nick's transparent! Light goes clean through him!"

That did it! In another moment all the girls had

tumbled out of the car and were prancing around the headlamps, fascinated and shocked by what they beheld.

Nick gave a regretful smile and glanced at Dawlish. The man's calmness was unshakeable.

"What does it mean?" Bernice demanded finally.

"It's a matter of mathematics, miss," Dawlish replied.

"Oh don't bother me with those! Can't you give it neat?"

"I can, miss, but I doubt if you'd believe me. However, from the look of the stars, and the fact that there are no shadows, I think we have unwittingly driven from three dimensions into four—or if not that, then into a sub-area of space which is very close to, but not actually a part of, our own space. Possibly it has its own time-ratio."

"Are you trying to scare the women?" Harley demanded.

"No, sir. I find it as uncomfortable as they do to be marooned in an alien space."

"Alien space be damned!" Nick said bluntly. "The obvious move is to drive back the way we came. We'll inevitably come to our starting point. Have we enough juice?"

"Just about, sir, but I must warn you that the effort is unlikely to meet with success. If, as I think, we have slipped into hyper-space, the chances against our passing straight out of it again are millions-to-one against. I could explain why, but it would take considerable time."

"Drive back," Harley ordered. "Only thing for it."

Dawlish shrugged and held the car doors open for the party to re-enter. Then he settled at the wheel, started up the engine, reversed the car, and began to speed down the empty road in the direction whence they had come.

Everybody was quiet, completely sobered. It was only as moment followed moment that they realized just how awful was the position. They had come into nowhere out of the normal everyday world and had not even glimpsed the point where they had crossed from the one state to the other. All of them being more or less ruled by their knowledge of the everyday, they were quite sanguine that the drive back would restore them to the point where the signpost stood near the church clock.

So Dawlish drove on and on, the miles flicking by on the trip-mileometer, and the road stretched between the endless fields. Endlessly, with never a break. And, as the trip continued with its six troubled passengers, the sky began to lighten considerably and the stars paled. Nick found himself looking for a moon, but could not see one.

"Dawn coming, or moon rising," he told Dawlish, finally.

Dawlish glanced at the dash-clock. "One-fifteen, sir, so it isn't dawn—unless Time here is very different. It's moonlight we can see, but not the moon itself."

"Why not? There isn't a cloud in the sky."

"We do not see the moon, sir, for the same reason

that we can't see shadows. In four dimensions light-waves do not obey the accustomed laws."

"But we can see the stars—I think."

"True, but do they look like stars, sir? No! They are like bars, their bases tapering off into nothing. Even their light is not as we are accustomed to seeing it."

Nick gave it up. He became moodily silent, like the others, watching anxiously for some sign of the road ending. None came, and after nearly an hour of swift travel the engine suddenly started missing, coughed, and finally died. Slowly the car came to a standstill and Dawlish put on the handbrake. "Petrol's finished," he announced.

Nick followed a line of thought and switched on the car radio. Rather to his surprise it presently began to operate, giving forth a dance band into the utter silence and milky glow of this weird land.

"Well," Nick said brightly, "we can't be so far off trail!"

"On the contrary, sir," Dawlish sighed. "One might receive radio quite clearly when millions of miles away in space, but it would not solve the problem of reaching the spot from which the radio program emanated!"

Nobody argued about this because nobody understood it. The dance band continued for a while, then the announcer spoke. "That concludes our dance music for tonight, and the time is now just upon midnight. We bid you all—"

The voice died away, and all the twiddling of knobs that Nick gave the set failed to restore it to life.

"That announcer's crazy!" Betty Danvers exclaimed. "It's long past midnight—twenty past two, in fact. For the love of heaven, what sort of a nightmare have we landed in?"

"If my guess is right," Dawlish said, thinking, "daylight should come eventually, and then we may be able to assess the position more easily. Until then I think we ought to try and sleep. The air is warm, we have plenty of rugs, and I took the liberty of preparing the picnic basket, sir, in case you decided on extra traveling."

"Extra traveling is right!" Nick commented dismally.

"Sleep?" Bernice repeated. "Under these frightful conditions I couldn't sleep a wink! Don't be so ridiculous, Dawlish!"

"I'm sorry, miss, but are the conditions so awful? We have peace all around us. Frankly, and with the greatest respect, I might say that I find things here more restful than in the ordinary way."

That awkward silence came back again. It appeared that, quite unobtrusively, Dawlish was taking things into his own hands—perhaps because he knew far more about the situation than anybody else.

Nick cleared his throat. "I think Dawlish has the right idea. Come on, girls, take the back seat, cover yourselves with the rugs, and do what you can to snooze. We men will take the front."

There were plenty of grumbles—but he was finally obeyed.

* * * * * * *

When Nick awoke again it was daylight and Dawlish's lean, immobile face was stooping over him. He was holding a plastic cup in which tea was steaming.

"Good morning, sir. Somewhat incongruously, I am afraid, I have here your morning cup of tea."

"Thanks."

Nick took it, hoping for the moment that he would find himself in bed at home with the satin curtains drawn back. But no! He was still in the car with a cloudless sky overhead and a considerable amount of heat beating down upon him from an invisible sun. It was the weirdest awakening he had ever known. Then he remembered the others and looked about him.

The girls were still in the back of the car, nibbling at the picnic sandwiches and balancing cups on their knees. They looked pasty, disheveled, and thoroughly miserable—even Betty Danvers, who usually managed to keep a bright smile under all circumstances.

Some distance away from the car, contemplating the landscape as he slowly turned on his heel, was Harley Brand. Now and again he scratched his head, then shrugged to himself.

"How's life, girls?" Nick asked, absently watching Dawlish busy with the small picnic oil cooker.

"Rotten!" Bernice declared with finality.

Nick drank his tea and surveyed. He could hardly have contemplated a more dreary panorama. Everywhere, save in the direction he took to be the east, were the endless fields of dry, brownish-green grass, flat as a billiard table, Nowhere a hill or moun-

tain. To the east, though, there was a curious gray blur that could have been a distant ocean. Otherwise, not a bird, not a movement, not a flower.

"I think, sir," Dawlish said, when the "breakfast" was about over, "that we should hold a conference. I'll ask Mr. Brand to join us."

Harley came over immediately and leaned on the edge of the car morosely, waiting for somebody to say something. Nobody did, except Dawlish.

"I think," he said, "that we can take it as an accepted fact that we have strayed into some space contiguous to our own. A fourth dimension does exist, but up to now it has only been in the realms of mathematics. But it is also a fact that other spaces and planes exist alongside our own, and now and again there is an overlap. As the ocean plunges its waves forwards and then retracts them, carrying with it driftwood which is borne out on the ebb, so other dimensions occasionally overlap our own and, by chance, somebody or something is perhaps picked up and drawn away on that ebbing, dimensional tide. Space within space, angles within angles, is the top and bottom of the Universe."

"Marvelous, for a chauffeur!" Nick declared, grinning.

"I still think we're on a circular road!" Harley insisted.

"That you can forget completely, sir," Dawlish told him. "The missing shadows, and absence of visible sun and moon in a cloudless sky is sufficient evidence of the fact that we are, at this moment, in a different

space from our own. Light has undergone a change, so probably has time itself—as witness the announcer last night telling us it was just on midnight when we knew it was twenty past two."

"But how did we get here?" Nick demanded.

"We may never discover that, any more than we can remember ourselves being born. We were shifted from one space to the other, and our only clue was the queer sound of the last note of twelve as it struck from the clock tower."

Nick gave a start as he remembered. "You noticed it too, then? A sort of cut-off effect?"

"Yes, sir. At that moment we must have crossed from one space to the other."

"But surely," Lucy Brand asked, "we can find our way back if we follow this road as far as it will go?"

Dawlish shook his head. "I'm afraid not. Just as one can never be sure that the waves on a shore will strike the same spot twice, so we cannot be sure of finding the way out. If we get out at all it will be by the merest chance; just as the merest chance brought us here."

There was dead silence—until Nick exploded.

"Dammit, man, do you realize what you're telling us? You are as good as saying we've got to stop here for the rest of our lives!"

"Yes, sir. I base my opinion on the fact that those who came here before us never returned to the everyday world."

Harley raised his head and looked blank. "Who the blazes ever came here before us?"

"Quite a few, sir. The records of missing people show that many thousands of people vanish every year without trace. Take two examples—Henry Potter of Maida Vale, who on the nineteenth of January, 1916, stepped back into his home to pick up an umbrella he'd forgotten, and was never seen again! Or the case of Dorothy Arnold of New York, who vanished from a busy shopping center in the middle of a summer afternoon. As for ships, they have disappeared in endless numbers and nobody has ever solved how, or why."

Harley straightened up. "So our names can now be added to the world's record of missing people? How very nice! However, we are pretty healthy at the moment, but what happens when the picnic stuff gives out? I've seen neither food nor water in this confounded place."

"Water there must be or grass would not grow," Dawlish answered. "We'd find water if we dug down."

"I'm doing no digging!" Bernice declared impatiently.

"Before long, Miss Forbes, you may have to do many things in order to survive. As for food, I think we have an ocean in the distance there, and it may contain fish. I think we ought to remove everything we need from the car and then bead towards that ocean—on foot, of course."

The women looked in dismay at their light evening shoes and costly dresses, the latter showing under the opened coats.

"Back to the primitive in one easy lesson!" Betty Danvers said finally. "Well, I'm game. Let's go, girls!"

But for her there would probably have been trouble with the grumbling Bernice and Lucy Brand, but against the younger woman's example they could not stand out, so they descended stiffly to the dusty ground and stretched aching limbs.

Nick clambered out too and joined Dawlish. Harley came wandering round the rear of the car and stood on the outside of the group, hands in the pockets of his evening trousers. He was unshaven and completely despondent.

"Rugs, picnic equipment, and stove," Dawlish said, handing out the various articles to one or other. "This is all we need. I am sorry to abandon the car, sir."

"Thirty thousand pounds down the drain," Nick sighed. "Ah well, we're still alive."

He began walking, dust stirring round his shoes, and as he went he slipped his arm through Bernice's so that she had to keep pace with him. She gave an angry glance.

"Things are bad enough without you looking so disgustingly cheerful!" she exclaimed.

"No use being miserable, Berny. If we're to die let us do it with a smile on our lips."

"The rugged individualist," Betty commented dryly. "Just the same, there's a lot in what you say, Nick. I know because I've tried it."

Nick frowned as the party struggled onwards. "Tried what, Betty? What are you talking about?"

"Myself, as usual." Betty gave a laugh. "This experience we have stumbled into is more amusing for me

than anybody because, even in the normal world, I wouldn't have lasted above six months."

The party halted, startled by the revelation. Betty had a defiant look on her pert face.

"I know all of you have got me down as a girl whose main abject in life has been to get rid of father's money," she continued. "But you've had the wrong angle. Since it doesn't matter much what we confess to each other I may as well tell you I've been having a last fling. Who wouldn't, with only six months to go?"

"You mean," Bernice asked in horror, "that you have only six months to live?"

"That's it." Betty shrugged and continued walking, her high heels catching in the rutted, dusty ground. "Something wrong with my heart. I heard about it six weeks ago, so I resolved to have the time of my life— and now look what's happened! I'm not the only one who's been given a death sentence! All of you have! Can you wonder I want to laugh?"

"But you won't, Miss Danvers," Dawlish murmured, coming up beside her with the picnic case in his hand and a rug over his shoulder.

She glanced at him quickly. She was noticing that he was far younger than she'd thought. No more than thirty-five.

"Why won't I?" she demanded.

"Because I think you are too generous-minded to laugh at people in the same boat as yourself."

Betty raised a critical eyebrow and said no more.

"After this," Bernice wailed suddenly, "I'll never

feel clean again in all my life!"

"If that's an ocean ahead you can take a swim," Nick said.

"Can I? In what?"

Nick hesitated, and then Harley Brand broke in: "I'm wondering how Consolidateds have broken this morning—"

"Dearest, it doesn't matter," Lucy told him patiently.

"What doesn't? Consolidateds matter a great deal—"

"You and Consolidateds may never meet again," Lucy went on. "Do try and get things in focus, Harley. We may finish up dying as savages, with no food, no clothes, and no hope. Your checkbook in your wallet will be so much waste paper."

"Rubbish! We'll return. Dammit, we've got to!"

"Which means we must have organization," Dawlish said. "Not so much for getting ourselves home, but for survival here. And organization demands a leader. I suggest—myself."

"Good enough," Nick said, before anybody could object. "You seem to know more about this mess than anybody, so it's only right. Okay, everybody?"

There were slow nods, nothing more.

CHAPTER TWO
SHIP OF THE DEAD

Halfway to the blue smudge on the horizon, which by now had taken on all the evidences of an ocean, a halt was called. One biscuit each and a small drink of cold tea was permitted, then followed a rest—particularly for the women who were looking jaded and smolderingly angry.

Then on again, and at last the first sounds in this silent, oppressive land became evident, sounds other than those the party itself was making. The growing roar of the sea, of breakers crashing on shore.

Towards four in the afternoon, according to Dawlish's watch, and checked by those of the others, the shore was reached. Utterly fagged out, the party sank down, close together, and Nick and Harley smoked half a cigarette each. Dawlish, being a non-smoker, was not troubled. He was gazing out to sea, weighing up the situation.

The sky was blue and empty, yet there was the definite heat of an unseen sun. No seagulls flew; nor was there a smudge on the horizon to reveal a distant ship.

"Dead," Bernice whispered hopelessly. "What did

we ever do to deserve being flung into a place like this?"

Presently Dawlish got up. He walked down to the tide line, mooched along it, and finally picked up some seaweed and studied it. He still had it in his hand when he returned.

"This is edible," he said. "Just as ordinary seaweed is if you know how to prepare it."

"Do you suggest," Bernice asked blankly, "that we should descend to eating seaweed?"

"Have you any other solution?" Dawlish asked politely.

Bernice opened her mouth and shut it again. She still had not fully realized that food had gone, that without something, no matter how unpalatable, death would inevitably follow.

"It will come out like cabbage," Dawlish added. "There is a good deal of driftwood with which we can start a fire. We have lighters; and, back along the route, we can dig down to fresh water. The picnic equipment will provide a makeshift saucepan. The brine is removed from the seaweed by constant boiling and change of water. When the cigarette lighters give out we shall have to resort to spinning a rod in our palms."

"I'll give a hand to get these things set out," Nick said, getting up.

Harley moved too and began to sort out the picnic tackle whilst Nick went back to the tide line with Dawlish to collect more seaweed. Amongst the women Betty Danvers spoke first.

"I suppose we ought to help," she said, pulling off her dustcoat and throwing it down. "Though I don't see what we can do."

"Go back along the road and get some water for these containers," Harley instructed, handing them over.

"And with what do we dig?" Bernice asked coldly.

"Your hands, Berny, and forget the manicure."

Bernice tugged off her heavy fur coat impatiently, then she snatched the container offered her and walked back up the shelf of beach. Lucy Brand followed after her and at last Betty went too. Harley watched them go, his lips tight. He was wondering what would happen if inclement weather suddenly descended. The need of a shelter was obvious, and he pointed it out to Dawlish as, with Nick, he returned with the seaweed.

"We'll build a bungalow, sir," Dawlish answered.

"With what? Sand?"

"No—trees. Look over there."

Harley and Nick turned. It was apparent to them now that the sea coast was formed into a bay some ten miles distant, and fronting the bay were cliffs. Capping this headland were masses of trees that probably stretched quite a distance ahead.

"So there is something besides grass!" Harley exclaimed.

"Evidently so. Naturally, if grass will grow in profusion then trees must too. We can easily get our timber from there. For the moment, however, we must concentrate on preparing our meal. Where are the ladies?"

"Gone to dig up water, as you suggested."

Dawlish said nothing. He began to break up the seaweed into one of the picnic containers.

"I'll help the girls." Nick said. "I fancy they won't be relishing looking for water."

He was right. He found the three women half a mile away lying on their faces, scooping to arms' length into the earth—and so far they had not reached water. But when Nick lent his aid, scooping far deeper than they could, the moisture at last began to become apparent, until ultimately there was enough of it to fill the two containers.

"Fresh, too," Nick said, tasting it. "That seems to prove it does rain here sometimes."

"Or else there are underground streams," Betty responded. "I'll bet we get pains after drinking this stuff, too."

"It'll be boiled," Nick told her, leading the way back to the shore.

When the water was handed to him Dawlish pronounced himself satisfied.

"Good!" he said. "The land behind being higher than sea level the water is bound to be fresh. There's a big billycan here. Fill it to capacity, please."

"After all we've done?" Bernice objected.

"I'm afraid so. Water is the most essential thing of all."

"Dawlish is boss," Nick said. "Better do it, girls."

"Meantime," Dawlish added, "we'll look for fish. I would be glad of the help of you gentlemen. The seaweed can start boiling."

Fortunately, there were fish in the ocean, of a small size and peculiar shape. Two hours later the party were seated on the warm sand eating the quite delectable fish and not too unpleasant de-salted seaweed. For drink there was only water.

"For some time to come, fish and seaweed are likely to form our staple diet," Dawlish said, when the meal was over. "At least let us be grateful for that much. We shall not starve. The next thing after that is to create a home, so we'd better take a look at that distant wood. We might even make our home there since one part of the shore is as good as another."

"But will there be water there?" Nick questioned.

"Should be. Soon find out."

The camping tackle was collected, coats were shouldered, and then the march began. The sand was too difficult to walk upon so they took to the hinterland, wandering across the dry, scrubby fields and towards the distant outcropping.

"It seems odd to me," Nick remarked, as they tramped, "that although there are fish there doesn't seem to be any other form of life. Is it just a Fish Age here, or something?"

"Probably a matter of light-waves and their behavior in this plane," Dawlish replied. "The fish, evidently, reflect light normally enough and so we see them. It is quite possible there are other forms of life about us at this moment but invisible to our eyes—as we are, probably, to them. On the other hand there is also the possibility that our physical form is such that we are

at this very moment walking through walls, and even people, without being aware of it. Just as it sometimes happens that beings from other planes walk through the midst of us and we sometimes catch a glimpse of them."

Nick looked startled, and then incredulous.

"Surely, sir," Dawlish finished, "you have now and again been convinced of somebody passing, or standing right beside you? A black shadow at the corner of your eye, gone the moment you try to look straight at it."

"Good heavens! I always put that down to liver!"

"By no means! Science tells us that at one time we were capable of actually seeing an extra dimension, so there must be a hangover left in our visual apparatus even yet. Science assumes that the red, fleshy piece in the corner of the eye is the vestigial remains of the more complex eye we once had."

Nick gazed about him. "If we are in the midst of people and buildings it's the best camouflage I've ever seen!"

"True, but remember nothing exists to the eye unless light produces it. Change the order of light, as it is changed here, and normal law no longer operates."

The subject was dropped—and a dimness that could only be interpreted as approaching night was coming over the face of things when the party finally reached the large wood perched high on the summit of the cliffs. The trees were of no species known in the normal world, possessing almost square leaves of gigantic size, and branches as rigid as pokers. There

were, amongst the smaller varieties, huge clusters of objects like hypertrophied grapes. Bernice eyed them enviously in the dying light.

"Think they're poisonous, Dawlish?" she asked, turning.

"Only way we can find out, miss, is to try for ourselves in a very small quantity, and see what happens."

"Damned dangerous!" Harley Brand objected.

"But inevitable, sir. However, since we can survive for the moment without food I thought we might select a site for our home. We can begin by hacking through these branches with the poor tools at our disposal—picnic knives and, if either of you gentlemen possess them—penknives."

Only he himself had a penknife, it appeared, so with this and the picnic knives a start was made. By the time night had come three massive branches, to form the main supports of the intended home, had been cut down. The site selected for the "bungalow" was just beyond the wood, on the headland, commanding a view of ocean and beach to the front, and the endless grassy wastes to the rear. And whilst the men worked on the trees the women used the plastic picnic plates to scoop out foundations.

Darkness brought a stop to activity. A meal of fish remains and a drink of water was the only nourishment at the end of it. Harley and Nick divided the last ciga-rette and smoked the halves morosely. Bernice pulled her fur coat up around her and started to doze. The silence became deathly. That was the one intolerable

thing about this plane—the awesome quiet.

And so, gradually, each one in the party fell asleep, and throughout the night there was not a ghost of a sound to disturb them.

Dawlish was astir the moment the first grayness came over the tranquil scene. Since, as leader of the party, he felt it his duty not to ask anybody to do something he could not do himself, he experimented with some of the giant grapes, eating the tiniest section and then going about the business of preparing breakfast whilst he waited for digestive reaction.

In fifteen minutes he had warmed up the last remains of tea in the vacuum flask and given it to the dully-stirring womenfolk. The men had to be content with water.

"With your help, gentlemen," Dawlish said, "we will have fish for breakfast. Come with me, please."

Nick and Harley struggled to their feet, yawned, felt at their stubbly faces, then followed the likewise unshaven Dawlish down the cliff slope to the beach.

"The water is warm," Dawlish announced, putting his hand in the gently lapping waves. "We can wash and catch fish at the same time. We can leave our clothes on. In this dry air it will not be possible to catch cold."

Nick and Harley nodded, none too eagerly, and pulled off their creased evening jackets. Then they waded out into the millpond calmness and finally took to swimming. It was not easy with the weight of clothes, but at least, it was refreshing. As for fish, they were in abundance and made no effort to escape, which was proof in

itself they had no reason to fear a foe in their domain.

As the men emerged, dripping, with fish in their hands, they caught sight of the womenfolk further up the beach, likewise sporting themselves in the water. Finally, it was a bedraggled-looking party in still damp clothes that squatted down to the fish breakfast, the fire of dry vegetation crackling brightly.

"Y'know," Betty Danvers said slowly, picking a fish-bone, "there's something queer about this place."

"You don't say!" Bernice exclaimed, astonished.

"I didn't mean it in that sense, Berny. I mean that there is something uplifting about it. I can't quite explain it, but when I woke up this morning it was with the feeling that I have never felt better in all my life. Sort of full-of-the-joys-of-spring feeling."

"Maybe something in it," Lucy Brand mused. "Perhaps because we slept in the open air. Makes a great difference."

"The explanation's simple," Dawlish said. "There are no vast crowds of people using up oxygen, no chemicals being ejected from industrial areas. I think all of us will find that the more we breathe it the better we'll feel. All the impurities will be cleansed out of us."

"Including tobacco juice and alcohol," Nick sighed.

There was silence for a while as the meal continued, then Dawlish said, "You'll find the giant grapes are harmless."

"Sure?" Harley asked, doubtful.

"Certain. I sampled part of one and suffered no ill effect." The others looked surprised, then Betty

Danvers gave an admiring smile.

"That took courage, Dawlish, and I think all of us should acknowledge the fact."

"Nonsense, Miss Danvers. Somebody had to make a test." The imperturbable way in which Dawlish referred to his gamble with poison had a sobering effect for a while and the meal was finished in silence—with grapes. Then Dawlish began moving. "We can make rapid progress with our bungalow today."

There were nods of assent, then Bernice stooped and tore a good six inches of costly material from the bottom of her evening gown.

"That's better," she said, kicking her feet. "I can't possibly work with all this stuff around me. You others should do the same."

Betty and Lucy did, finishing up looking like schoolgirls. The men glanced at one another. The surprising thing was that any of the girls—and Bernice in particular—should really want to work. Usually they did their best to avoid it.

And work it certainly was as the invisible sun rose higher in the cloudless sky. Its beating heat-waves enveloped the six as they toiled back and forth in and out of the wood, carrying the necessary branches and gigantic square leaves with which it was proposed to thatch the roof. By approximately noon the four corner posts and floor were in place and the grimy party broke up for a meal.

Then, once again, each one of them was secretly astonished at how much they could accomplish without

feeling tired. Dawlish, though, was a sensible leader and did not allow work to proceed beyond the tea period. When the meal of cold fish and water was over he spoke thoughtfully.

"Gradually we are dropping into a kind of timetable, and we don't feel exhausted because of the wonderful air. However, in future we'll take the evenings to ourselves, to do as we wish—walk, swim, laze, or whatever it may be; and the day we'll divide into work and foraging for food. We can combine business with pleasure by taking walks and looking for good sources of food at the same time. We shall also need another source of water as our present supply is running out. I'll have a look for some this evening."

"I'll help you, if I may?" Betty volunteered.

"Delighted," Dawlish smiled.

"I'm going to look for something to work as a razor," Nick decided. "This blasted beard tickles."

"And I'm going to find a weed as a substitute for tobacco," Harley said. "I'm half dead without nicotine."

"With you men out of the way we girls can fix our clothes to look more in keeping with this desert island set-up," Bernice said, glancing at Lucy Brand.

"Okay," Dawlish responded. "We'll be on our way, then."

He turned, Betty at his side, and for a time they walked in silence. Then the girl laughed slightly.

"I could do with sharing your amusement, Miss Danvers," Dawlish said, glancing down at her.

"Any reason why you can't use my first name?"

"Every reason. Our social stations are different. You are the daughter of a wealthy industrialist and I am a chauffeur."

"You mean that you were, and I was. Values have changed completely, Dawlish. You are the commander of our little band, and the rest of us put together haven't a quarter of your brains."

"I'd hardly say that, miss."

"Oh, call me Betty, for heaven's sake." She gave a half reproachful glance of her blue eyes—and for perhaps the first time Dawlish noticed that they were not the customary pale blue which matches red hair, but brightest sapphire.

"Betty, then," he responded. "Since values have gone overboard you might as well know I answer to 'Horace'."

"I'll call you 'Daw' for short," Betty smiled. "As to my laughter just now, I was thinking what sights we both look. What would they say in Mayfair or Park Lane?"

"I'm afraid I'm not very interested as to—ah, this looks like a good spot to find water," Dawlish broke off.

Betty promptly went down on her knees beside him and began to scoop at the dusty, sandy earth. Just here the dry, withered grass had thinned out, which made the task of burrowing down considerably easier.

At the end of fifteen minutes of rough digging the first sign of water appeared. Dawlish unslung the billycan from his back and, by degrees, filled it. Then

he hauled it back onto his shoulder and stood up.

"We know where to come in future," he said. "This spot is easily distinguishable by the bare earth, to say nothing of the hole we've made. Which seems to finish our tour."

"Still daylight," Betty reminded him. "And we might have a look if any small animals exist."

"True. Come along, then."

Whether or not Betty stumbled deliberately Dawlish did not know, but when he held out his hand to save her she kept it there, imprisoned against her waist by her arm.

"I'm a girl who says what she thinks, Daw," she remarked, as they strolled onwards in the warm, sunless evening.

"So I've noticed."

"I've a great admiration for you. That isn't just flattery: it's the considered opinion of a girl of twenty-five."

"Thank you," Dawlish murmured, looking out to sea—and then suddenly he stopped, staring at the distant horizon. For a long time he remained gazing at a remote speck. Betty could see it too now, but it made her vision dance to try and hold it in focus. It seemed so far away.

"A ship!" Dawlish breathed. "Just drifting on the current—and headed this way! I'll swear it's getting larger."

He moved forward urgently and Betty clung onto his arm. They settled down in the grass perhaps a quarter

of a mile from the edge of the cliffs and fixed their gaze on the growing speck. The tide was apparently flowing and was carrying the vessel towards the shore.

"Not a very big one," Dawlish said presently. "Looks like an old tramp steamer, or something."

"Do we go back and tell the others?" Betty questioned. "It seems to be heading more to the left than here, which ought to bring it to the shore not far from our base."

Dawlish got to his feet quickly and helped her up. They went back to the base camp at a run, to discover that the others had already seen the vessel and were standing on the beach, watching it and waving.

"Waving to that ship is rather a waste of time," Dawlish remarked to Betty. "Obviously nobody is aboard or they'd stop themselves drifting."

"I—I've just discovered something!" Betty exclaimed, her eyes widening. "Despite that run we made I'm breathing more or less normally."

"Is that so remarkable?"

"It is for me, with a wonky heart."

"Evidently, the pure air and exercise have done you good. Now let's inform these good people their war dance is useless."

Dawlish led the way down to the beach with Betty coming up in the rear. There was time to notice that Bernice and Lucy Brand had altered their evening gowns so that they now resembled sarongs, that Nick had mysteriously shaved himself, and that Harley was smoking something in a roughly fashioned pipe. The

odor it gave off was reminiscent of pineapples, or amyl acetate.

"That ship is unmanned," Dawlish announced, and the four turned in surprise. Then they all began to speak at once.

"We saw it from the hinterland," Betty explained. "But Daw doesn't think it's going to be much use to us, and he ought to know."

"Why set the man up as a paragon?" Harley demanded, with uncommon viciousness. "I'm getting sick of all this kow-towing to Dawlish!"

"I'm sorry, sir," Dawlish said, surprised. "On the whole I thought my leadership was satisfactory."

"We're not a bunch of damned children!" Harley objected. "As for that ship, if it can be manned, what's stopping us doing it? Maybe we can sail out of this hell-hole to somewhere sane."

There was a strained silence; then Lucy spoke up.

"I know you've a rotten temper, Harley, but you can at least keep it to yourself. We've got to be civil with each other if we're to maintain any kind of peace."

"If you can keep calm under these conditions, Lucy, you are either crazy or hypocritical! It just can't be done! The silence! Seaweed for food! Water to drink! I can't stand any more of it—"

Harley swung round, intending to depart, evidently no longer interested in the approaching ship and thinking only of the base camp—but Dawlish stopped him.

"Just a moment, Mr. Brand. What's that you're

smoking?"

"What's that to do with you? You're a non-smoker!"

Dawlish was unmoved by the glare in Harley's curiously glazed eyes.

"I happen to be interested, sir, non-smoker or otherwise."

"It's filthy stuff," Nick put in. "I tried some and I felt as though my head had blown off. It's some kind of weed Harley dug up out of the wood undergrowth."

"And poisonous," Dawlish said deliberately.

Harley took the pipe from his teeth and looked at it. For a moment he seemed startled, and then he scowled.

"Keep your blasted opinions to yourself, Dawlish!"

"Whilst I'm the leader of this party, sir, I can't allow you to poison yourself. You are smoking an acetate of some kind, and from the smell of it amyl is mixed up in it. The fumes, directly inhaled, are poisonous. Throw that pipe away."

"What!" Harley exploded. "By what damned right do you—"

In one stride Dawlish reached him, snatched the pipe, and hurled it into the oncoming tide. Harley breathed heavily, his face darkly tinged with color; then he suddenly lashed out his right fist. Before it could land he received a blow under the jaw that flattened him on his back in the sand.

Harley scrambled to his feet, intending to hit back, but instead he gripped his middle, profound anguish on his face. Immediately Lucy was at his side.

"Harley, what's wrong?" She put an arm about his

shoulders. "Can't I help?"

"Yes. Get me back to the camp. I've got to lie down. I've the devil's own stomach ache."

He turned, doubled up, and shuffled along the sand with his wife at his side. Dawlish raised an eyebrow and there was a hard smile at the corners of his mouth.

"He's going to be deathly sick," he commented, as Nick, Bernice, and Betty looked at him questioningly.

"Can't we do something for him?" Bernice asked.

"Unfortunately we have no medical kit. He'll be all right, but let that be a lesson to all of you. Don't eat, drink, or smoke anything unusual until you've asked me. If I can't give an opinion I'll try myself first."

"I never thought I'd give up smoking the hard way," Nick growled. "Better than that horrible stuff, though—"

"Look how near that ship is!" Betty broke in excitedly.

The others turned. The light was beginning to fade, but it was still sufficient to show that the tempest-battered tramp steamer was now no more than a mile away and drifting steadily inshore.

"We could swim out to it," Bernice said. "That's why Lucy and I fixed our dresses like this—so we can go in and out of the water any time we want without extra weight."

"We'll wait for it to come to us," Dawlish decided. "It won't be very long."

His guess was right. Just as the darkness was descending the ship's keel grounded in the sand and

the vessel became motionless, on its side, the water lapping against its barnacled plates.

None of the quartet wasted any time. Led by Dawlish they climbed up the ropes dangling from the vessel's listing side and so gained the deck. It was weatherworn and battered and had obviously not been cleaned for an unimaginable time. Some of the planks indeed were rotten with age, which, added to the steep slant of the vessel, made movement difficult.

Whilst Dawlish examined the empty wheel-house and found only maps faded with age, the others scoured the desk, noting that only one lifeboat, in fair repair, remained in the davits. By the time this investigation was complete the darkness had descended and the rod-like stars were smeared overhead.

"No use looking below without lights," Nick said, as they decided what to do next.

"Might be oil in the lamps," Dawlish replied,

They found their way to the nearest companionway and descended into the depths. They felt their way along a narrow passage and so came to a door. It opened stiffly under Dawlish's pressure and there was black void beyond—or at least almost black. The more the four stood peering into it the more their eyes became accustomed, and presently they could discern the blurred gray circle of a porthole and, beyond it, a dim view of the starlit beach.

Dawlish began to advance slowly into the gloom; then he paused, peering at something round and white near the porthole. Bernice, immediately behind him,

gave a cry of horror.

"It's a skull!" she gasped. "A skeleton seated at the desk!"

Once the first shock was over it was discovered that there were two other skeletons as well, one on the floor and the other slumped on a chair in a corner. All trace of clothes had long since gone.

"This ship's been lost for a long time," Nick commented. "We'd better come back in the daylight, Dawlish, and see what there is."

"Yes, sir—but in the meantime there is much we might learn from this logbook."

Dawlish picked it up from the desk, feeling dust thick upon it, and disturbing the hand of the skeleton in order to do it. Then he led the way out of the cabin and returned to the fresh air under the stars. Sobered, Nick, Bernice, and Betty followed him down the swinging ropes to the sand and they returned to their base camp. Here Lucy Brand had started a fire with her husband's still operative lighter. Harley himself was lying on his wife's fur coat, squirming and twisting, then relaxing for a while and gasping.

"For God's sake can't you do something for me?" he demanded of Dawlish, noticing him in the firelight. "I'm dying!"

"Once you have been sick, sir, you will make rapid recovery," Dawlish assured him. "Cold comfort, I'm afraid, but then the conditions are extraordinary. You will be interested to know we found the steamer's logbook."

"I'm not the least interested."

Dawlish shrugged and turned aside. He lay down near the fire and opened the logbook to study it. Around him, Betty, Bernice and Nick also stretched themselves.

"The *Mary Newton*!" Dawlish exclaimed at last, when he had succeeded in deciphering the faded name written in ink on the logbook.

"Never heard of it," Nick said.

"That isn't surprising, sir, unless you happen to be a student of unusual phenomena, as I am. She is only one of dozens of missing ships on Lloyd's list. She was last seen near the Cape of Good Hope in brilliant summer weather on the tenth March, 1930. She never reached port and was never heard of again—so she was added to ships like the *Cyclops*, the *København*, and others that have vanished without trace. She was bound for Rio to pick up a cargo of meat, but never accomplished her purpose."

"And there she lies," Bernice muttered.

Dawlish turned the pages of the logbook slowly and found most of the earlier entries illegible with age; but later ones were clearer. The last one was significant by reason of the wavering pen stroke at the finish....

'Have tried all normal means of seamanship to determine our position, and failed. Distant coastline is not positioned on our charts. Stars do not check with normal maps. The last of the water has gone. I fear an early disaster. Some of the crew have taken to the boats. How we got here I do not know and—"

"They sailed into it, and we drove into it," Betty said. "Which seems to prove you can get caught up just anywhere."

"Just as I said," Dawlish responded. "And this bears out my earlier theory that we are in a plane very close to but not a part of our own space. If we're lucky we might get out of it as simply as we came into it—but my belief is that we are faced with a lifetime here and must make the best of it. At least we can abandon the building of our bungalow. That ship will make a perfect home for us when we have tidied it up and removed the skeletons."

"There's only one thing against that," Nick said. "Using the ship as a home, I mean. Suppose one night when we're asleep a storm and a big sea gets up? We're liable to be carried away to heaven knows where!"

"Would that matter so much?" Betty asked. "We haven't the remotest idea where we are anyway."

"It would matter," Nick answered, "because we might die on board if we didn't reach land. Water and food would run out, whereas here it cannot. No, I prefer to stay on solid ground even if it is unfamiliar."

"I think, sir, you may be right," Dawlish conceded. "Though the climate seems pretty equable, we cannot rely on it. At least we may find tools on that ship which will help us with our bungalow work. In the morning we can make a thorough search. In the meantime, may I ask a question?"

"Shoot," Nick invited.

"You have shaved quite effectually. May I ask how?"

Nick grinned and from his trouser pocket produced a sea shell, not unlike that of an oyster in shape, but much larger. The edge was serrated.

"Sharp as glass," he explained, handing it over. "It will even shave me without lather, though I don't know how long the 'blade' will last. In any case there are thousands of them on the beach."

Dawlish tested the shell on his own beard and the effect was magical.

"Thank you, sir." He handed the shell back. "I shall lay in a supply for myself. Queer, but even here one feels the need to conform to civilized tradition—if one is clean-shaven, that is."

"Well," Nick, said, getting to his feet, "I think I'll take a stroll before turning in. Coming, Berny?"

He held down a hand to her and she rose up beside him.

CHAPTER THREE
BERNICE DISAPPEARS

It was peculiar how, in this plane, the night never seemed to become really dark, and the glow could not be entirely attributed to the moon.

"Probably refraction of light waves," Nick said, surprisingly, as Bernice brought up the matter.

"Could be," she agreed, and became silent for a while as the stroll continued. The immensity of the thing that had happened was such that the human mind could not adapt itself to it immediately. At the very outset of the adventure there had been the feeling that everything would work out right—that this was only a temporary diversion into something abnormal—but now hope was dying. Civilization, as such, and all its amenities—money, comfort, influence—wiped out. Bernice found it peculiar to reflect how selfish her outlook had been up to now.

"You and I are engaged, Nick," she resumed presently. "I don't suppose we intend to stay permanently in that state, so what happens if we want to marry? Who's going to perform the ceremony?"

"Seems to me that Dawlish is the only answer."

"Dawlish! But he's only a servant—"

"There you go again, Berny! He's the captain of this little band of ours, and a captain has the right to perform a marriage ceremony. Yes, he's the one to do it. I think there might be a Bible aboard the *Mary Newton*, which will give the authentic touch."

"Well, why not tomorrow? No sense in delaying, is there?"

Nick did not answer. He had come to a halt and was standing with his attention sharpened, as though listening to something. Bernice frowned as she studied him.

"What's the matter—?" she began, but Nick raised a hand for silence. For a long time he was motionless, then at last he relaxed and rubbed the back of his head ruefully.

"I'm going cockeyed," he announced. "I could have sworn I heard people talking."

"Talking! Who? Where?"

Nick looked about him in the pearly gloom. "Sounded to be a lot of them. I couldn't make out what they were saying. The craziest thing of all is that one of them sounded like Henry T. Mythorn himself!"

"I think," Bernice said seriously, "that it's time we got back to base and had a sleep—or at last you should. When you hear voices in the wilderness it's time to quit!"

Nick did not answer. He turned about, took Bernice's arm, and they began to stroll back the way they had come. He did not mention the matter of the voices again

in case he sounded too ridiculous, but he was quite convinced in his own mind that he had heard them—and said so to Dawlish when he returned to camp.

Dawlish was doing his best to sleep when the information was given him. It was vital enough to make him sit up sharply. Some distance away Harley Brand was vomiting and groaning.

"Voices?" Dawlish repeated. "You're sure?"

"Sounded like it. It's crazy, of course."

"Not necessarily. It may be a point where this plane overlaps the normal world and the barrier between is so thin that sound waves carry across it. It may even be a point we can investigate with a hope of getting out of here! You'd better show me."

By this time, Betty Danvers—not properly asleep anyway—had also awakened. She scrambled up hastily from under her dustcoat and followed Dawlish, Nick, and Bernice as they strode swiftly into the night. Lucy Brand looked after them for a moment, puzzled, then gave her attention again to her husband.

"About here," Nick said finally, when he had returned to the approximate spot. "Doesn't seem to be anything at the moment, far as I can hear."

Dawlish, however, was not satisfied with this. He roamed slowly around in the gloom, his ears cocked. Nick and the two girls wandered in a narrow circle, not quite knowing what they were going to hear—if anything at all. Then Betty Danvers stopped and retraced a few steps.

"Here!" she gasped. "It's absolutely uncanny!"

Immediately the others were at her side. All four of them motionless, catching gusty drifts of conversation as unreal and remote as something on the astral plane. Here and there a sentence or two became "detached" from the general murmuring and made sense.

"...night club of his makes a packet of money...."

"...that she is, but she's selfish, concentrates only on her own pleasures...."

Then a woman, clear and distinct for a moment— "If you ask me, she's only going to marry Nick Clayton for his money. That painted hussy hasn't an unselfish bone in her body!"

"That's me they're talking about!" Bernice gasped, amazed. "I don't recognize the voices, but I'll swear it's one of those old hags at the house-warming!"

"Can't be!" Betty protested. "That was a couple of nights ago—maybe more. How could we hear it now?"

"Echo?" Nick suggested—then as mysteriously as they had made themselves evident the voices faded into silence as the weird, shifting barrier between planes intervened again.

"Interesting," Dawlish commented, moving around in an endeavor to make contact—and failing. "In fact the most interesting thing that has happened so far. At this point the veil is extremely thin."

"Yet immensely strong." Nick sighed. "Otherwise we could walk straight through into the normal world."

"Let me see, now," Dawlish mused, looking about him. "We traveled, when on the road, almost to the point where the village would have been, when the

petrol gave out. It is quite possible that our movements in this plane have conformed to the movements we might have made in the normal plane, which would have brought us to the vicinity of Mythorn Towers, Mythorn Towers being the only house in the district where people are up and about—the rest of the village being asleep—it is the only place from where we can hear voices."

"It's crazy!" Nick objected. "We've lived some days and nights since then—"

"Time outside may be almost stationary compared to here," Dawlish pointed out. "Don't forget that radio announcer."

"Do these voices give us a better chance of getting home?" Betty asked flatly.

"I wouldn't say that," Dawlish replied guardedly, "but at least it does pin a certain familiar section in the outer world—and around that we can, by degrees, form the rest of the parallels with our own environment. The village, the road up which we came, and so on. We can return at intervals and see if any more voices reach us."

He said no more. Instead he searched around until he found a piece of stone. Returning with it he dumped it in the spot where the voices had been heard.

"So we'll know it again," he explained. "Now we'd better get back to base and catch up on some sleep. We've a lot to do tomorrow."

Because he was the leader Nick and the two girls followed obediently behind him but each one of them,

as they tried later on to sleep amidst the disturbance created by Harley Brand, was thinking nostalgically of those weird voices—and of home.

* * * * * * *

The following morning Harley Brand was normal again. Looking very chastened, and as though suffering from a bad hangover, he apologized at breakfast for his behavior of the previous night, even though he had obviously only a hazy recollection of what had happened.

"Lucy told me I was a bit of a boor," he said uncertainly, as the group sat around a meal of fish, ship's biscuits, and canned meat, with which the *Mary Newton* had been found to be plentifully supplied.

"Forget it," Dawlish said, shrugging. "You can't be held responsible for what you do under the influence of a drug. I only hope you won't try smoking that stuff again."

"I'm cured," Harley sighed. "I don't want to smoke anything any more. Tough way to reform, but it worked. Come to think of it, I don't need this either."

He pulled his wallet from his pocket and examined it. Within it was about three hundred pounds made up in various denominations of currency.

"Hold it!" Nick advised him. "We may be nearer to escape than you think. Destroying that money might give you a thrill, but it would haunt you forever if we found our way back home."

Harley hesitated and frowned. "Back home? How?"

He was told of the voices, then to add flavor Dawlish produced a rough map he had made. He laid it down so everybody could see it.

"I was awake early and drew this," he explained. "First I explored the *Mary Newton* and found this food—and there is a good deal more too, which being canned should be all right for us. Then I drew this map. The dotted lines represent the normal world, and the others this plane we're in. A kind of superimposition."

"According to this map, then, this place here— where we have our base—is about two miles beyond the village of Little Brook," Bernice said.

"Yes, Miss Forbes. And across here"—Dawlish indicated the dry grassland extending away infinitely from the base camp—"is the lane up which we traveled in the car, and lost ourselves. At the remoter end of it is the signpost where we turned off and into this incredible plane. I think we should mark each point with stone and by that means we can approximately position where we are in relation to the outer normal world."

"What's the good?" Harley growled. "We can't get back."

"We might one day," Dawlish answered. "Anyway, it can do us no harm to stroll, even in imagination, through the world we once knew. Even to hear the voices coming from there is a stimulus."

"If we went far enough we'd contact London, I suppose?" Betty enquired.

"I imagine so, by moving eastwards."

The meal progressed, then Harley seemed to have a change of heart.

"All right then, I'll mark out the positions after breakfast. Suit you, Dawlish?"

Dawlish nodded. "You take the map. You'll need it. We'll continue the building of the bungalow. There are tools on the ship there, just as I'd hoped. I suppose you ladies will help us?"

"Definitely!" Betty declared, getting to her feet. "And incidentally, Daw, are you anything of a doctor?"

He smiled. "Why? Do you need first aid?"

"No, but I'd like a check-up on this heart of mine. I've already told you I feel tons better than I did, and I'm still feeling that way. I want to know if it's a fluke or a permanency."

"Why bother?" Dawlish asked, shrugging. Then he got to his feet actively. "Well, we've work to do. Let's get started."

As usual he was obeyed. Harley set off on his mission to mark out the landscape and those left behind transported tools from the ship and then turned themselves into builders. By dinner time the floor of the bungalow had been completed, and by early evening one wall was up. Bernice set herself the task of preparing the evening meal over the ship's transported oil stove, near which was a newly opened drum. On the stove the frying pan was busy. Fat sizzled as freshly caught fish browned appetizingly.

The meal was eaten and enjoyed and, as usual, conversation began to float into desultory channels;

then Dawlish got to his feet in readiness for recreation.

"I think I'll take a stroll," he said.

"I'll come with you," Betty said promptly.

Bernice glanced at her and then asked a question: "Dawlish, are you capable of marrying Nick and myself?"

"I imagine so. After all, there are only ourselves to consider and if we all agree that that shall binding, then so be it. A Bible would help, though."

"Here," Lucy Brand said, handing one from behind her. "Bernice found it today on the ship."

Dawlish took it, then glanced at Nick. "I take it you are agreeable, sir, as the other party?"

"Well, yes, but—"

"But!" Bernice exclaimed, staring. "What in the world do you mean?"

"I—er—I'm not trying to slight you in any way, Berny, but what if we find our way back home unexpectedly? We shall then no longer be legally married."

"Surely that's simple enough?" Harley asked in surprise. "You'll get married again in the ordinary way."

"I don't think we should," Nick said uncomfortably.

Bernice set her mouth. "You've always led me to believe we'd get married."

"Right enough, but just consider. Dawlish performs the ceremony and we become man and wife. Suppose a child followed? Let's assume we're in this place for ten years.... How do we explain, if we accidentally get home, that we need to get married when we have a

child of ten with us?"

"Scandal and muck-raking," Betty sighed. "Wouldn't the columnists love it? And they'd pick on you, good and hard, because you're worth so many millions."

"Exactly. And they wouldn't give Berny much peace either. I think we should be absolutely sure that we're stuck here for life before we make a move."

Bernice did not say anything. She turned and walked languidly away. The others watched her—a slim, brown-legged figure in her ragged, makeshift sarong, blonde hair tumbling to her shoulders.

"I agree with your viewpoint, Nick," Lucy Brand said.

What Dawlish thought nobody knew. His face was as impassive as ever. Hands in pockets, he wandered away in the opposite direction to Bernice, Betty quickly catching up with him. When they arrived back it was growing dark and to their surprise Bernice had not returned.

"You didn't see her when you were strolling?" Nick asked Dawlish urgently.

"No, sir. Not a trace."

Nick hesitated no longer. He set off in the direction Bernice had taken. It was not a difficult thing for him to do, for in the sand, and later the dusty soil, the girl had left clear impressions of her bare feet. The gentle glow showed the trail distinctly and Nick began to follow it at a half run, worried that the girl should be out alone in this weird land now the night had come.

He followed her imprints for about a mile and a half,

which brought him to a massive stone. Upon the stone was roughly chipped the word SIGNPOST. Harley Brand had put it there in the morning to mark the approximate spot in the outer world where the signpost stood. And the odd thing was that Bernice's footprints stopped here, in mid-trail! There was nothing but the night and the gentle hot wind.

"Berny!" Nick yelled. "Berny, where are you?"

There was no answer, save the distant murmur of the tranquil sea. The girl had vanished and there was no conceivable place where she could be hiding, otherwise her footprints would have led straight to it. There was only the infuriating, rod-like stars, the grayness, and the impalpable distances curving over the edge of beyond.

Nick swung and began to run, arriving back at the site of the bungalow like a whirlwind. His very speed and anxiety brought the other members of the party to their feet.

"Gone, you say?" Dawlish caught at Nick's shoulder and forced him to calm down a little. "You're sure?"

"Of course I'm sure! Her footprints stop in the middle of empty landscape, by Signpost Rock."

Dawlish asked no more questions. He began moving instead—at a run, with the others hurrying behind him. When the rock was reached he gazed down thoughtfully at the sudden cessation in the footprints. He looked about him, up at the bewildering stars, and then sighed.

"Good for Miss Forbes!" he exclaimed at last.

"Good?" Nick repeated blankly. "But what in—"

"She must have found her way back," Dawlish interrupted. "Not by any effort on her part. Somehow, by reason of the incomprehensible laws controlling this plane and the normal one, she must have stepped out of one into the other."

Nobody spoke. The shock was stunning, all the more so because the transition had apparently been accomplished so easily. Yet so had the transition of the car.

"Then we've lost her!" Betty's mouth sagged in amazement.

"Yes. But it's encouraging. If it happened to her it can happen to us, and the vital spot seems to be around here somewhere. This is where the overlap of the two planes is most marked. It is near here where we hear the voices, and it is here where, in the ordinary world, there stands the signpost that marked the beginning of our journey here. Miss Forbes has got back: maybe we shall sometime."

Nick made a gesture of annoyance. "This business makes one realize how limited our intelligence really is, otherwise we'd know what to do to get home. As it is we just step gingerly into the air and nothing happens. Why?"

"Because our senses do not incorporate a knowledge of four dimensions, sir," Dawlish explained. "We only understand how to move in three. Just as a worm only knows two dimensions, length and breadth."

"I have the feeling that I am to blame for this," Nick muttered. "If I'd agreed to marry her she wouldn't have

wandered off. All would have been well."

"A queer viewpoint, sir, if I may say so," Dawlish commented. "Not so very long ago you were hinting at Miss Forbes' selfishness: now you reveal the same tendency yourself. Surely she will be happier in natural surroundings than here?"

Nick said nothing. Hands in pockets, he considered, mooching away slowly. It was Harley's voice that made him pause.

"Just a minute, Nick! There may be a way of discovering where Berny is—or at least if she got back safely. What about the ghostly voices? I haven't heard them yet, and I'd like to. Surely the first place Berny would go would be Mythorn Towers?"

"That's right!" Dawlish exclaimed quickly. "This way. The spot is marked."

He led the others to it, half a mile distant, and sure enough as they came into the area the five could distinctly hear the ebb and flow of words and the deeper background of many more voices.

"I don't get this," Nick said. "It can't still be the housewarming guests talking! Another day and night have gone past for us!"

Nobody answered: they were too busy concentrating and trying to hear. They picked up odd snatches.

"...and of course that wonderful car of his. I'm not saying anything against Nick Clayton, mind you—he's one of the best in the world—but I do believe he thinks money can buy anything and—"

Drift, a babble like an ill-tuned radio, then sharp

sentences again predominating.

"...Henry T? Oh, he's more money than sense, otherwise he wouldn't have bought a white elephant like this."

None of the conversation was consecutive. Bits and pieces, mainly the senseless, ill-natured comments of a band of everyday people drinking and murmuring in holes and corners. Nowhere a mention of Bernice.

Finally Nick wandered away and the others joined him. The quiet seemed appalling after the voices.

"Evidently the voices are heard better at night than by day," Dawlish mused. "I wonder if the sun has anything to do with it?"

"Dawlish, will you please realize something!" Nick implored. "Those viper-tongues are still wagging at the house party! How in blazes does it come to be still going when we're nearly five or six days ahead of that period?"

"The unequal balance of Time-ratio, sir, as I said before. Here we must be living with terrific speed, but are not aware of it because we've nothing by which to judge. Relativity. Everything is relative. Take speed: you can only judge velocity by its relation to the fixed objects around it."

"Then we are listening-in to a time before we ourselves vanished, and certainly long before Bernice got back?"

"I would say, sir, near as I can judge, that we are listening to the time after we left the house-warming—since many of the references concerning you and Miss

Forbes have been in the past tense—but whether the time is before our actual moment of crossing from one state to the other I don't know."

"How long before we catch up with hearing if Bernice has got back?" Lucy Brand demanded.

"I have no idea."

Again the impasse, the feeling that everything was utterly hopeless; yet it was balanced by the thought that perhaps at any moment one or other might follow in the wake of Bernice and step unexpectedly back into the living world where people, however shallow their natures, would live and breathe again and the sounds of normal life would come back into the quiet.

"I'm going back to the bungalow," Nick said abruptly.

Turning, he ambled away through the grayness. Harley and his wife soon began to follow, but Dawlish was prevented from doing so by a tug on his arm from Betty. He could see her young, pretty face in the dim light, her eyes reflecting the incredible rod-like stars.

"It's not time to turn in yet," she said. "Can't we walk a bit? I love doing that: you talk so intelligently."

Dawlish laughed. "I have met few girls who like a man to talk intelligently! Usually they are more interested in hearing him talk about them."

"Strange man that you are," Betty sighed, holding onto his arm and glancing at his powerful profile against the sky. "You manage to keep yourself so much to yourself—and yet you are still sociable. I think that's wonderful."

"If we stay here for the rest of our lives you'll find it

getting monotonous, Betty."

"No—never!" She was quick in her denial. "You'll always have something fresh to say, always some new corner to turn, no matter how long we stay. Even in the ordinary way I always knew you were a cut above the lounge-lizards amongst whom I mixed, only I didn't dare say so then. I can now and it just doesn't matter. So I can be grateful for being flung into—wherever we are. And my heart, too: that's miles better. I keep on telling you that, don't I?"

"You still sound very young, Betty," Dawlish replied, with an affectionate clasp of her shoulders. "Please don't have any false illusions about me. All you've got is a bad attack of hero-worship."

"At twenty-five? Oh, no! I got over that in my teens. I also learned then to speak my mind—and I'm doing it now. I'm in love with you, Daw. Surely you can see that? Not only with you for yourself, but your knowledge, your calmness, your leadership—"

"In fact the perfect paragon!" Dawlish laughed. "No man is that, Betty—but thanks all the same. And please don't go overboard for me completely. It might be difficult to live up to it if we happen to follow Miss Forbes back to where we belong."

"It wouldn't change my opinion, or my intentions—ever." Betty had come to a halt, completely resolved. Dawlish stood looking down at her for a moment, then he took his arm away from her shoulders and kissed her.

When they returned to base they found Harley and

Lucy half asleep, propped against the edge of the bungalow floor. Nick was seated not far away, chin on hands as his elbows rested on his up-thrust knees. He was looking up towards the stars as Dawlish and Betty approached him.

"Got over it yet, sir?" Dawlish enquired, settling down close by with Betty beside him.

"I've no choice," he answered. "Anyway, something else has taken my attention. Take a look at those stars there—"

Dawlish and the girl glanced up and then started. For the first time since they had arrived in this quiet, calm land the stars were misted over, and as the moments passed they slowly began to disappear. From the sea a fresh wind began to rise, gathering in strength as the moments passed.

"Evidently the climate is not always perfect here,' Dawlish said quickly, getting to his feet. "Storm of some kind is blowing up, and as we've no means of knowing how violent it may become we'd better get to shelter quickly."

"Where, for instance?"

"The *Mary Newton*. Since we haven't finished building the bungalow it's our only sanctuary. Collect everything you can find."

Dawlish hurried across to the dozing Harley and his wife and shook them into wakefulness.

"Now what?" Harley growled, then he spat and spluttered as dust and sand grains blew into his face in the wind.

"Storm coming," Dawlish explained quickly. "We're going to the ship. Bring all you can grab."

Almost before they had gained the listing side of the beached vessel the storm broke in all its fury with a whiplash of lightning and vicious crack of thunder. At the same instant the gathering breeze changed abruptly to a gale, and from a gale into a hurricane. The speed at which the storm developed, and the demoniacal fury it possessed, was startling.

Led by Dawlish, the party blundered down the companionway into the cabin that had formerly been the captain's. Here there were oil lamps ready for use in just an emergency as this. Dawlish lighted them with the ship's matches and then looked around him in the yellow glow. Betty, Harley. Nick, and Lucy were all present, listening in some alarm to the screaming of the wind. In this cabin all seemed safe enough, and the skeletons and other traces of age had long since been moved out.

"I have the uncomfortable feeling," Nick remarked presently, "that nothing is going to remain of that bungalow floor into which we put such labor!"

"That isn't entirely what's worrying me, sir," Dawlish told him. "My fear is that perhaps the wind will blow away those stones we've set to mark our environment. If so, we'll have extreme difficulty in locating the exact spots again. We might be near, but not dead on—which is as good as being infinities away. Particularly now we know Miss Forbes' vanishing point."

As he finished speaking Dawlish looked up with a

start as with incredible fury the real force of the storm broke.

It had little parallel in the outer world, save perhaps in tropical climes. The wind shrieked until it was deafening, and the sea driven before it was also on the flood, which brought monstrous breakers thundering in-shore—which presently battered against the side of the beached ship. Glancing about them in alarm the party could do nothing but wait and see what happened. Through the porthole they had a vision of surging ocean and lightning-ripped sky.

It was not long before the thing Dawlish had feared began to happen. The ship started to quiver and vibrate as it slowly began to right itself in the surging waters. Finally it straightened up with a dizzying heave, setting the five staggering helplessly. Nick was the first to reach the porthole when the initial lunges had abated slightly.

"We're heading out to sea!" he exclaimed. "Or at least we are on the move—carried by currents, probably."

Dawlish lurched over the swaying floor and joined him. Outside the breakers were creaming inwards to the shore and smashing themselves against the bow of the cliffs that formed the bay. The tidal currents at this point prevented the vessel from being tossed onto the beach: instead it rode the waves and began to move outwards into the storm.

"We're getting further away from land every moment," Betty said anxiously, peering through the

porthole. "What do we do?"

"Try and guide the ship," Dawlish replied, swinging round. "I don't know the first thing about seamanship, but if the helm still answers and the wheelhouse is intact we might manage something. Better come with me, sir," he added to Nick. "It may take two of us."

They hurried from the cabin and up the companionway. The wind smote them in a solid blast when they gained the deck. The only advantage was that it was not particularly cold, otherwise in their half-clad state they wouldn't have been able to stand it.

Clinging to each other, and whatever projections they could find, they fought their way to the wheelhouse—but before they could enter it a gigantic wave reared, hovered, and then smashed down upon them. They were flung from their feet and slithered along the deck, hitting the rail with numbing force.

Dawlish scrambled to his feet with difficulty and helped up Nick. They lurched and reeled helplessly as the deck seemed to swing up and down beneath them.

"No use, sir, I'm afraid," Dawlish panted. "We'd better get below while we're in one piece. Another wave like that might break up the wheelhouse and us with it."

They abandoned their effort and, inch by inch, crept back to the companionway, and so below. Harley and the girls looked up expectantly.

"No use," Dawlish said, closing the door. "We'll have to drift."

Nobody said anything. Each seemed to be thinking

what to do next. Then after a while Betty appeared to realize something and she moved to the porthole and peered through it.

"Storm's dying down!" she exclaimed, turning eagerly. "The lighting's ceased and I don't hear any thunder—but from the look of things we're a long way out on the briny. I can't even see the shore any more."

Dawlish joined her. Nick, Harley, and Lucy threw themselves in chairs and relaxed, waiting. Dawlish gazed out onto the pearl-gray semi-dark outside and all he could see was the gray face of slowly calming waters. The shriek of the wind had gone, and so had the rolling of the vessel. It began to look as though the unearthly calm normal to this weird region was beginning to reassert itself.

"Yes, the storm's practically ceased," Dawlish admitted at length. "We'd better go up on deck and look around."

He opened the door for Betty as she kept beside him and then followed her above. As abruptly as the storm had broken so it had now vanished. There was not a breath of wind and the sea was rapidly returning to its normal millpond quietness.

CHAPTER FOUR
ISLAND OF LOST SHIPS

"Queer," Dawlish commented, as he gazed upon the calming scene. "Evidently, storms in this region are as crazy as everything else. We've moved some distance, too. Land's out of sight."

There were sounds to the rear as Harley, his wife, and Nick came up on deck. They looked about them, then up at the magically cleared sky. The rod-like stars were visible again.

"Think it's ebb tide?" Harley asked, joining Dawlish.

"Perhaps. On the other hand it may be some kind of undercurrent that is moving us along. No reason why we shouldn't try and steer. Safe enough now to go to the wheelhouse—"

"Just a minute," Lucy interrupted, peering into the distance towards which the ship was heading. "What do you make of that?"

Everybody gazed in the same direction and gradually began to discern what Lucy meant. There was apparently a big stretch of dark land ahead, or at least something marring the smooth surface of the pearly sea. It was only as the vessel moved nearer to it, pulled

by inexplicable currents, that the "island" began to assume outlines. There were curiously straight trees with cross bars on them: tilted spires at all manner of angles: great up-thrusting dark hulks

"Ships!" Nick gasped, astounded. "Dozens of 'em! All piled up into one complete island!"

"Right," Dawlish confirmed, gazing fixedly. "An island of lost ships, all drawn there by the tidal current, in which we are now caught. And that's where this ship will finish, too!"

His guess was right. The speed of the old ship had accelerated now and with its rivets and plates creaking it ploughed through the water towards its doomed sisters. In a matter of fifteen minutes it had reached them. The party stood back from the deck side, prepared to run for safety as the ship plunged into the midst of the rearing, rotting vessels and huge overhanging masts.

There was a monstrous ripping sound, the chaos of age-old timbers and metal plates crumbling and snapping, then the *Mary Newton* came to rest solidly locked in the island of derelicts.

Nick drew a deep breath. "Whew! That's better! I half expected we'd get buried under this junk pile."

"This region must extend for miles," Harley remarked, turning slowly and seeing nothing but lofty, lopsided masts, and here and there a diagonal funnel. "What do you make of it, Dawlish? Is this the shipping of this plane—all that remains of it—or did it come from elsewhere?"

"If by 'elsewhere' you mean the outer world, sir,

then I think it came from there," Dawlish answered. "It seems that in this plane there is a kind of common whirlpool into which unmanned vessels are drawn. The *Mary Newton* was evidently an exception and had steered clear of it, until the storm drove her into it. Or maybe the storms themselves are the motive force which finally drives every ship to this graveyard."

"Well, I—" Nick began to say, and then he gave a start. He just could not go on speaking because he was too astounded, so he gripped Dawlish's arm and pointed.

Dawlish saw what he meant: so did the others. In this utterly deserted land a bright light was shining some distance away! Even more extraordinary, it was swinging hack and forth and coming nearer.

"Some—somebody else alive!" Betty gasped, clinging to Dawlish. "Gosh, I know I shouldn't be scared, but I am!"

Dawlish was silent, watching. Occasionally, as it advanced, the light made jumps as though the person holding it leapt from one hulk to another. Then came the sounds of his progress, the ring of his boots on metal—and at last he himself took on outline in the pearly glow. He came nearer still, and at last was only a few feet away on the neighboring vessel, a hurricane lamp swinging in his hand. He held it high and peered forward.

"Well I'm scuttled!" He exclaimed in amazement, his voice rusty as though he had had little need to use it. "Living people!"

He seemed to consider it a quite impossible revelation. So, whilst he gazed and muttered to himself, the party on the *Mary Newton* studied him. He was attired in a tattered seaman's uniform, apparently that of a captain, and possessed a great mane of unkempt gray hair and a flowing beard and moustache. In physique he was not particularly big, but his shoulders were massive. His eyes, lighted diagonally by the oil lamp, had a fixed, staring quality as though he had been suddenly awakened from a deep sleep.

"Who are you?" Nick called out.

"English!" the apparition yelled. "Sweet oil of Judah, he speaks English!"

He lunged forward suddenly, leaping to the *Mary Newton*. Then he grabbed the hands of the party each in turn and began a fandango, the oil lamp bobbing on the curved wire about his wrist.

"Cap Bronson isn't alone any more!" he kept chanting. "He's got company! That'll drown out the nasty noises."

"Eh?" Betty asked, surprised.

Captain Bronson suddenly stopped dancing and put a finger to his bearded mouth with exaggerated caution.

"You'll wake 'em," he said, peering about him. "The ones who sleep—down there." He sank his voice and turned one finger downwards dramatically, indicating some subterranean region.

"Crazy as a bed bug," Nick murmured, as Dawlish stood beside him.

"Let's get something straight," Harley said brusquely.

"Are you Captain Bronson?"

"Right!" Bronson yelled, with a wild flourish. "Cap Bronson!"

"From where? Have you a ship around here?"

"A ship, he says!" Cap Bronson looked around hint with a wild glint in his eyes. "A ship! Sweet oil of Judah, I've thousands of 'em! Pick what I like, take what I like. I'm the ruler, don't you see?"

"No," Lucy said politely.

"A woman," Bronson whispered, staring at her. "And another one here!" He looked at Betty. "I'd forgotten what they looked like. All I have had has been a picture of my wife and kid. She must be twenty-two now. Hell! That's what it's been! Hell! Twenty-two years of it! No, twenty! Madge was two when it happened— Noises!" Bronson screamed, wheeling around him and looking nowhere in particular. "Noises, noises! And the fish! They come out and look at me, blast their mainbraces!"

Dawlish took Nick's arm and led him on one side. In somewhat embarrassed silence Betty, Lucy, and Harley watched Bronson go into another of his capering dances, the lamp swinging up and down.

"The man's half crazy," Dawlish murmured. "If he is speaking the truth he's had twenty years in this ghastly plane, and that's enough to break any one person. Solitary confinement would be a summer vacation by comparison. If we handle him carefully he may be useful. He must know a thing or two about the environment, having been here so long. What is more, he is a seaman and can perhaps steer us back to the shore

we've lost. We certainly can't do it ourselves."

"Right enough," Nick agreed. "And he must have access to food and water to have survived— Okay, let's see what we can do."

Dawlish moved forward again and spoke quietly, causing Bronson to pause in the midst of his jig.

"If you have a moment, Captain Bronson, I'd like a word with you."

"If I have a moment!" Bronson bellowed with laughter. "I've been dry-docked here for twenty years and he asks me if I have a moment—! Laugh, blast you!" he commanded, seeing the serious faces.

"I'm Horace Dawlish," Dawlish said. "The leader of this party. We're stranded, same as you are—and we don't know how we got here."

Bronson was silent. He had quieted for the moment, but his eyes were constantly darting about as he listened. By degrees Dawlish gave the whole story, finishing with a negative shrug of his shoulders.

"So there it is, Captain. We're completely lost. We wondered if you could perhaps guide this vessel of ours back to the shore from which it was snatched?"

"That," Bronson answered, stroking his magnificent beard, "takes a lot of consideration. How do we drive this thing? We don't have the women behind the stern pushing, do we?"

He burst into apoplectic laughter at this, but Dawlish remained perfectly calm.

"We might rig up sails," he answered. "If we can move this vessel from the jammed ships around us it

is seaworthy enough to make the trip back. Don't you see, Captain? If we can only return to our lost shore we stand a chance of getting through to our own world again. And that would include you!"

"Back—back home?" Bronson hesitated, looking vague. "But that just isn't possible. I've been here twenty years and—"

"There's a scientific answer to all this," Dawlish insisted. "If any man can get you back home again, I can. But not until you behave like a mariner and get us on the move."

Bronson was silent for a while, then his flourishing began again.

"Right!" he yelled. "Right it is! I'll do it! I'm the best seaman that ever was, and what do I get for it? Noises! Fish come and look at me and we'll dine first," he finished, without any pause to change the subject.

"Gladly," Dawlish smiled. "We haven't had a meal for some time, nor have we slept. We're pretty well exhausted."

"This way, all of you! Follow the lamp—the only bright thing in a dark world."

Bronson scrambled to the side of the ship and leapt outwards with superlative ease to the next wreck. Dawlish followed him and then caught the two girls as they landed. Nick and Harley followed quickly afterwards. Thereafter the party kept in the rear of the half crazy old seaman as he led the way across the hulks that formed this forgotten cesspool of shipping. Bronson sang as he went, with a force sufficient to awaken the

dead.

It was during the seemingly interminable journey from ship to ship that Dawlish noticed something in the gray light, and he stopped suddenly. He pointed to a nearby vessel lying on her side, most of her falling to pieces.

"The *København*!" he exclaimed. "One of the most famous of missing ships! Now we do know we're in the land to which ships and people have disappeared."

"Course you are!" Bronson had caught the words and came back to look at the *København's* prow. "You'll find 'em all here—the *Cyclops*, *Saint Augustine*, *Pride of Alaska*—all the ships that ever disappeared from maritime records without trace or explanation. Like mine did. I was skipper of the *Baltimore Belle*. If you know your records you'll remember it was sailing for the States, then something happened—I dunno what. We just went on sailing but didn't get anywhere, and finished up here."

This was the most rational statement Bronson had made so far. Perhaps the presence of other living beings was having a steadying influence upon him.

"And your crew died?" Betty asked.

"Of thirst. We sailed for maybe three months and I was the only one who stuck it out. Some jumped overboard, some died horribly from lack of food and water. I was about dying, too, when a storm sprang up—sweet oil of Judah, I was being flung into this mass of craft before I realized it. But I'd come back to life. The rain slaked my thirst, and once I got this far I found water

and food, particularly on some of the other vessels. I was alive—and I'm still alive after twenty years. Understand?"

"It's a miracle," Harley said. "Twenty ears in this solitude is enough to drive anybody—" He was about to say "mad," but Dawlish stopped such a tactless blunder by cutting in.

"How did you know we'd arrived, Captain? Were you on the watch?"

"I heard you. You couldn't drive that ship of yours into this mass of hulks without making a din, could you? I knew something had happened—but I didn't expect people. But come on! We're wasting time!"

So, presently, Captain Bronson's abode was reached. It was a heeled-over ship, about a mile from the *Mary Newton.* The party followed the mariner across a listing deck to a companionway. Once they had descended it they found the entire interior of the ship had been taken to pieces, leaving one huge chamber as large as a ballroom. In this, obviously taken from the other ships nearby, was every conceivable type of furniture and most of it good, though ancient. In fact, the quarters of Captain Bronson were the last word in comfort. Even the floor had costly rugs, evidently taken from state-rooms and lounges.

"Sit down, sit down," Bronson invited, waving his hand, and the five obeyed, glancing about them in the glow of the six oil lamps fixed at different positions on the walls.

"You've evidently plenty of oil," Nick remarked, as

Bronson busied himself in the distance, preparing a meal.

"All the oil I need. Much of it crude stuff taken from the dozens of engine rooms in this island. Last me another twenty years if I need it. I've everything I need, even to this galley I'm working on now. Arranged everything myself. Not bad, eh?"

"I don't know whether to laugh at him or sympathize," Betty murmured, seated next to Dawlish.

"Don't do either. In a case like his one chance word on the wrong side might turn him vicious—"

"Whispers!" Bronson yelled, glaring. "That's what I don't like! Whispering voices! Nasty noises! I hear 'em nearly all the time—'cept just here. Always quiet here."

Nick gave Dawlish a glance. "Say, do you suppose he's talking about the voices we heard?"

"Hardly the same ones, but possibly something similar," Dawlish answered—then when Bronson brought forward six plates on which lay splendidly cooked fish, it seemed the moment to ask a question.

"Tell me, Captain, what kind of noises?" Dawlish's manner was entirely easy.

"Nasty ones! They hurt! Honkings, grindings, whistles— Like being in the middle of traffic! Drives me crazy to hear it. That's why I'm here, so I don't hear it."

"And the voices?" Dawlish questioned.

"All kinds. Men's voices—and women's." Bronson's look became far away for a moment. "I used to listen. I used to think I might hear my wife, or my daughter.

I even thought I was dead and listening to the living. Now I know differently. Those voices are in me, and I'm probably crazy."

"Those voices actually exist," Dawlish said deliberately. "We have heard them too—all of us, but they'll be different from the ones you heard. Do you know what you really heard?"

"I've told you! Voices!"

"The voices of people in London," Dawlish explained. "And the 'nasty noises' as you call them probably belong to traffic. At a rough guess I'd say that around here we are approximately in the center of London, superimposed upon it."

"Superimposed?" Bronson was mentally wrestling, his brows knitted. "How d'you mean?"

"A matter of dimensions, Captain. Let's eat while I tell you."

"Right!" Bronson swung away to the galley with its oil cooker and returned with two freshly baked loaves and a percolator full of coffee. Yet another journey he made to bring cups, saucers, and condiments, then he had everything set out on the big central table.

"Plenty of supplies," he said, seeing the surprised looks. "Most of it in air-tight bins. Flour, coffee, cocoa, beans, tea, everything. I can bake my own bread, can't I? Start eating if you don't want to slight me. Now what's this about dimensions?"

Over the meal, quite the nicest the party had had in this strange plane, Dawlish made the facts clear. Or at least as nearly as he could with Bronson's intense stare

pinning him.

"You're a madman, sir!" Bronson declared finally, slamming his fist on the table. "How could a ship or a car move into somewhere else without there being a reason? What do you take me for?"

"It's the only logical explanation," Harley Brand snapped. "If you'd any blasted sense you'd realize it!"

Bronson sprang to his feet, his eyes blazing. "Insult me at my own table, eh?" he shouted. "First a pack of lies about voices and noises, and now you slang me because I don't believe you— You're all up to no good! You're like the fish that are always popping up and looking at me. They'd laugh in my face too, if they could. Why? Because I'm trapped here! Trapped and damned!"

"We're all in the same predicament," Dawlish said.

"Get out!" Bronson ordered. "All of you! And quick!"

Nobody moved, realizing how absurd the situation was. No man would order away his guests just because of a comment of which he did not approve. Captain Bronson was plainly very abnormal in his outlook.

"All right," he snapped, as the party remained at the meal. He swung away to the wall and before anybody had grasped his intention he had taken down a ready-oiled and loaded rifle. Carefully he put it to his shoulder.

"Just a moment," Dawlish said quietly, rising. "Aren't you being just a little foolish, Captain? We can show you the way to get back to your wife and daughter. That's what you want, isn't it?"

Bronson hesitated, a sympathetic chord struck; then

his face hardened again. "You're probably lying about that, same as everything else. Why should I trust you? Why should I trust anything when a filthy twist of fate threw me into this hell-hole for twenty years? I can only speak at all because I've talked to myself so long. You hear? To keep me alive!"

"Why?" Dawlish asked. "There can only be one reason why you have kept yourself alive—and that's because you believe you will one day find your wife and daughter again. Right?"

Bronson put away his rifle, his mood reversed.

"Right! Yes, I know—you think you can help me find them. All right, I'd be a fool to prevent you. Forget what I did just now: I'm out of touch with my fellow men—and things."

He sat down again at the table and for a moment held his head in his hands. Then he suddenly grasped the percolator.

"Coffee?" he asked, and started to pour it.

Dawlish, who felt he was beginning to get the hang of the man's peculiar temperament, ventured another question.

"Would it be too personal to ask your age, Captain?"

"Blast it, no. I'm seventy, I suppose."

"Not a bit of it," Nick laughed. "About fifty, I'd say."

"I said seventy!" Bronson shouted. "I was fifty when I was wrecked, so I must be seventy now. I haven't forgotten how to add up!"

Dawlish mused for a moment, then said: "Captain, you expect when you find your daughter to discover

she is twenty-two, don't you? And your wife twenty years older than when you last saw her?"

"If they're not dead," Bronson sighed.

"You will probably discover," Dawlish finished, "that your wife is hardly a day older and that your daughter is still two years of age."

Not only Bronson, but Nick, Betty, Lucy, and Harley all looked astonished at this pronouncement.

"That's absurd!" Betty protested.

"No." Dawlish shook his head. "I've been convinced of something ever since we came into this plane, and that is that we are timeless. If not that, then our rate of. metabolism is exceptionally slow compared to that of the normal world. I base my theory on the fact that the voices we have heard all exist at the period when we stepped out of the normal world—just before midnight on the thirtieth of June. Then there was that announcer saying that midnight had yet to come."

"But we keep living day by day and night by night," Harley objected. "That's time, isn't it? We use up energy and need food to restore it. All that must happen in a period of time."

"Time, of all scientific definitions, is the vaguest," Dawlish replied. "It is purely a method of measurement to prevent chaos. But it is more than probable that in a fourth dimension, such as we are in now, Time undergoes a vast alteration and bears no relation to the Time we know. We are existing in a kind of suspended space wherein we grow no older though we seem to live and move normally. Outside this plane Time is more or less

a continuous Now, that Now being the instant when we left it."

"Then everything that happens here, even if twenty or thirty years ago, isn't really happening at all?" Betty asked, her eyes wide.

"It's happening all right, Betty, but in relation to the Time of the normal world it occupies perhaps only a split second. The two states are utterly different from each other."

Nick reflected. "I was never much good at science, but I do seem to remember reading somewhere that, granted another dimension, we could probably accomplish the work of a lifetime whilst a clock struck one note. I. thought it crazy, but maybe it wasn't."

"Time," Dawlish said, "is only the movement of a body through space. You cannot move anywhere in space without Time. Therefore, if the nature of space is changed, as it is in the fourth dimension, the time-factor related to it is changed also."

"You know your science, mister," Bronson said, as though he were talking to his first mate. "I'm sorry I ridiculed you earlier on."

"Is there any reason," Nick asked, "why we can't try and break through into London since we're in its vicinity? Why go back to the other spot?"

"Because we know that Bernice managed to return home at that spot. It might never happen in this particular position."

"We'll get on our way as soon as it's light," Bronson decided. "Meantime we'll finish our meal and then

bunk down for what's left of the night. Plenty of furniture in here with which you can manage."

So once the meal was over everybody, including Bronson, found a comfortable spot, Betty and Lucy taking over Bronson's own big double bed, and some sleep was obtained before the shadowless daylight appeared in the portholes. Then came the luxury of a razor for the men, and for the women the joy of a completely equipped bathroom.

Once breakfast was finished the party moved up to the listing deck. The air was still and warm and in the daylight it was surprising to discover how far the island of lost ships extended. But for Bronson it would have been next to impossible to find the way back to the Mary Newton.

He seemed to be in a much more rational mood as he led the way with agile leaps from vessel to vessel. Presumably, on the previous night, he had been so thrown off balance by meeting human beings he had not been able to stay coherent.

"Well, here it is," he said finally, as the *Mary Newton* was regained. "Steam-driven, blast it! I could have managed with sails. Now I'm not so sure."

"She's not jammed very tightly," Nick said, studying the position. "Just her nose held by this wreckage in front, but she's made a clear passage for herself to the rear. Do you think if we had enough ropes we could act as tugs and pull her out? Like they do with barges?"

"Barges!" Bronson echoed, blankly. "You call this a barge, sir? Fifty or a hundred of us couldn't pull it!

Ridiculous!"

Dawlish smiled dryly and Nick looked discomfited. Then Betty said, "If nothing grows old in this region why shouldn't the boilers still work? And incidentally, if nothing grows old, why are all these ships wrecks?"

"Because of the force with which they arrived, young woman," Bronson retorted. "Sweet oil of Judah, that should be plain enough. It's an idea about the boilers, though. Let's take a look at 'em."

He jumped across to the trapped vessel, the others scrambling behind him, and then they went down into the stokehold. There was an interval whilst Bronson lighted the hurricane lamp he had brought with him, then they peered around them in the ill-lit gloom.

"No use me looking," Dawlish said. "I don't know a thing about a stokehold, or ship's navigation."

"Landlubbers, the lot of you!" Bronson snorted. "I'll soon tell you." And he moved away to study the equipment. "Yes, not so bad," he said finally.

"You mean we might get steam up?" Harley asked.

"No harm in trying. Give me a hand."

There was no hesitation as far as Nick and Dawlish were concerned, They worked under Bronson's orders and prepared the furnaces. In half an hour they were in action and Harley and the two girls, out on deck, stood watching the clouds of filthy smoke pouring out of the funnel and drifting away across the wilderness of wrecks.

"It would have been an even quicker job if you'd lent a hand," Betty reminded him.

Harley shrugged. "I'm not turning into a stoker for anybody! No reason why I should with Nick and Dawlish willing to do it."

"The fact that all of us have to do our share doesn't occur to you, I suppose?"

"I've done mine—and the longer we're in this plane the more I see the uselessness of trying to get out of it. If we ever do escape it will be by accident, not design. In the meantime I refuse to work like a laborer."

"Hey, you!"

At the roaring voice of Bronson, Harley turned languidly to see the mane and massive beard projecting from a nearby companionway.

"Speaking to me?" Harley asked.

"Who in blazes else did you expect? There's a rope trailing over the side. You and the women grab hold of it and as I put the screw into reverse pull on the rope. It'll swing the ship slightly round and save us fouling that wreckage to port."

Bronson vanished again and Harley tightened his lips. Betty gave a cynical smile.

"You have your orders, mister," she said. "Let's get busy, Lucy. Harley's probably too important to soil his hands on a rope."

For once Lucy followed Betty instead of her husband. She vaulted lightly over the side of the vessel after Betty had led the way. They found the rope easily enough, seized hold of it, and waited for something to happen. Then, looking rather shamefaced, Harley scrambled down and joined them.

"I was—" he started to say, but Bronson's powerful voice from the half-wrecked wheelhouse atop the bridge drowned him out.

"Hold it, not play with it!" he yelled. "Quickly! We're under way."

Harley, surprisingly enough, did as he was told. Bronson sounded the siren for no particular reason, then there was a rattle and grinding as the propeller started to revolve. It gathered revolutions, churning up filthy water and striving to tear the tramp free of the imprisoning wreckage.

"Pull down there!" Bronson bawled. "Pull!"

Amidst a grinding of wreckage the ship began to move backwards. Straining until they were nearly bent double the trio braced their feet and had the satisfaction of seeing the vessel just miss the fouling wreckage which could have stopped its progress.

"Right!" Bronson yelled. "Come aboard, you three."

Realizing they might be left behind, the trio moved faster than they had ever done in their lives before, scrambling to the deck as the vessel began to glide away towards more open water. Breathless, they stood looking about them.

In a matter of minutes the vessel had drawn clear of the wreckage entirely and, still traveling in reverse, was edging out to the open sea. Once he reached it Bronson turned the vessel about and she began to glide forward into the millpond.

"Well, we're on our way," Bronson shouted from the bridge. "Or we will be when we know where we're

going. Where is this land supposed to be?"

"That way," Harley answered, pointing into the misty distance. "You can't see it now, but that's the direction."

"How do you know?"

"I remember the curve we took when heading into this wreckage."

"Right!" Bronson turned back to the wheel; then he bawled orders below—to Nick in the engine-room and Dawlish in the stokehold. The vessel began to increase speed, leaving a creaming wash in which unique fish bobbed and leapt, much to the fury of Bronson.

"Blasted fish!" he raved. "Always coming out and looking at me! Makes me feel like a curio."

"Curio is right," Lucy murmured, leaning against the deck side and watching the water surge by. "At least our eccentric friend seems to understand seaman-ship— And I hope you got the direction right, Harley."

He looked surprised. It was the first time his wife had ever questioned his judgment.

"Dead right!" he retorted. "You'll see."

He was evidently correct, for after perhaps half an hour of cruising a distant purple smudge showed up on the horizon. Bronson kept steering steadily towards it and, by degrees, the outlines of the bay came into view, and then the cliffs and the beach where the bungalow floor had been laid. But there was no sign of it now. The beach was completely empty.

CHAPTER FIVE
RAIDERS OF THE AIR

"I'll have to beach her," Bronson called down, after studying the situation. "Nothing else for it."

He sent a warning down to Nick and Dawlish whilst the trio on deck waited intently for the moment when the tramp would strike the sand. It came at length, the vessel heeling over and flinging Harley, Lucy, and Betty across the deck. They began to pick themselves up as Bronson came down from the bridge. In a moment or two Nick and Dawlish also appeared.

"Good!" Dawlish exclaimed, his eyes gleaming. "Right back where we started. Many thanks, Captain."

Bronson looked around him in some bewilderment. "Sweet oil of Judah, d'you mean to tell me you prefer this desolate bay and beach to my headquarters? Is this all we have after the trip?"

"Soon build a new bungalow," Dawlish told him. "Tools are aboard this ship. The most important thing of all is to see if the signposts we put in different places have survived. Come along, everybody."

He led the way down the rope ladder that Bronson tossed over the side. Very soon each member of the

party was heading back to the approximate spot where the bungalow foundations had been laid. But as they had expected, and seen, not a trace remained—except for four sunken holes where the side posts had stood.

"So much for that," Dawlish sighed. "We'd better see if the signposts are still in place."

They were not. Evidently the force of the wind in the recent storm had completely removed them.

"No sign of the footprints Bernice left behind either," Dawlish commented, studying the ground. "Rain and wind have obliterated them."

"All we can do is approximate the spot," Nick said, and began to study the situation, Captain Bronson standing close by and muttering under his breath.

Dawlish began to move back and forth, trying to locate that spot where he had heard the voices of Mythorn Towers, but either he was a long way out in his calculations, or else the overlap of planes had changed, for he could detect no trace of sound from the normal world.

"Begins to look as though we've lost contact," he said, as the group collected together again. "The approximate spot where Bernice vanished is here"—he tossed down a stone to mark it—"and I only hope it's correct. Unfortunately, approximate isn't good enough in a case like this."

Betty looked about her and sighed. "It's mighty hard to think that around here is the open country, and a lane with a new signpost, with a church opposite it." Then as she saw Captain Bronson looking at her fixedly she

added in haste, "In the normal world, I mean. We're just a fraction away from it, yet that fraction makes it as distant as the North Star."

"And as unreachable," Nick added. "Well, moping around here isn't going to do us any good. We'd better get back to the woodland and start rebuilding that bungalow. Do you wish to stay with us, Captain, or sail back to your island home?"

"Dammit, I've got to stay!" he roared. "How do I get that tramp back without help, and if you come with me how can you stay here?"

Crazily though it was put, the observation had logic, so without further comment the party returned to the beach where the *Mary Newton* was standing and, for a while, they were busy transferring from it all the food-stuffs and other essentials. By the time the job was done it was dinnertime—canned meat, canned pota-toes, and coffee.

"Since one doesn't grow old here," Betty said, as the meal progressed, "it would explain perhaps why my heart seems to be all right. I mean, since I was only given six months to live, I'll never die because I'll never become six months older!"

"But we must be getting older!" Harley insisted. "The very fact that we keep on using up energy and replacing it with food and sleep is surely proof of that?

"We're getting older, yes," Dawlish agreed, "but not in relation to the outer world. And as far as this plane is concerned we are getting older so very slowly it is hardly noticeable— It's so utterly complex to explain,

involved in the mathematics of time and space. Let's just accept it."

"No choice," Nick said. "And I wonder how Berny's faring?"

Lucy smiled somewhat wistfully. "By now she'll be back in Mayfair, I suppose. Warm baths, perfume, soft bed to lie in, servant to wait on her, everybody listening to her amazing story and none of them believing it. I don't know whether I envy her or not."

"Not!" Betty decided. "I still stick to my view that I like this primitive life better than the other one. We've no worries, no money, no responsibilities. The only thing that might spoil it, far as I am concerned, would be absence of men—but I haven't that to worry over. Have I, Daw?"

Dawlish only smiled and after studying him reflectively Lucy said, "I think we're all improved. Even you, Harley."

"Thanks!"

"I mean it. You've grumbled a lot, of course, but on the other hand you haven't broken into violent tempers or threatened to break my neck."

Harley looked uncomfortable under the eyes of the others.

"He often used to threaten that," Lucy explained. "I'm glad we came here. He's been so compelled to stay beside me he is beginning to recover something of the attentiveness he had to begin with. He lost it when he started making money."

"Money's no good to anybody!" Captain Bronson

declared. "Threw mine away long ago— Causes no end of trouble. In fact it's a—" He stopped, staring so fixedly at something to the rear that the others finally turned and looked too.

"Bernice!" Nick gasped, dumbfounded.

It was Bernice, only a few feet away—but she was not the neat girl in the sarong who had walked away in a temper. Her sarong was ripped in several places, her hair was tangled, and there were deep scratches on her bare arms and legs. That she was on the point of exhaustion was obvious for even as she came forward her knees buckled beneath her and she fell senseless in the sand.

Immediately Nick and the other men were at her side. They lifted her gently and bore her over to the region where the meal was laid. They lowered her to the tarpaulin they were using as a groundsheet and borrowed Betty's dust coat as a pillow.

"What do you make of it, Dawlish?" Nick asked, puzzled, glancing up from bathing the girl's forehead with seawater. "She's all in, and from the look of things she's been in the devil of a mess. Thinner, too. Hasn't had a meal for lord knows how long, I imagine."

Dawlish did not attempt to answer at that moment. Instead he concentrated on the task of restoring Bernice to consciousness.

"Here, give her this," Bronson said brusquely, handing over a flask of ship's rum from his pocket. "That'll do it."

Finally he did the job himself and as the fiery spirit

trickled into her mouth Bernice began to revive, coughing and spluttering at the same time.

"Th-thanks," she gulped at last, her senses fully returned. "I-I passed out, didn't I?"

"Afraid you did," Nick agreed. "So did we, pretty nearly, when we saw you back again. Where have you been?"

Bernice held her head in her hands for a moment. She gave a little shudder as though the recollection of the things that had happened to her was nearly too much to bear.

"Let me have something to eat," she said at last. "And a drink of coffee. I've not had anything since I was last with you."

The food and coffee were promptly forthcoming and the party gathered round the still shaken girl as she ate and drank ravenously. When she had finished her strength seemed to have returned considerably and more color had come into her cheeks.

"Where did you think I'd gone?" she asked. "From your conversation when I came upon you I gathered you thought I'd found my way back home?"

"Everything pointed to it," Dawlish responded, puzzled. "You had disappeared, and your footprints had vanished abruptly. There was no possible spot to which you could have jumped, so we naturally assumed—"

"I was carried away," Bernice interrupted.

"Carried?" Harley repeated. "But the footprints just vanished—"

"A bird!" Bernice cut in, close to hysteria. "The

biggest bird I ever saw! Raiding from the air! It came swooping down just as I was walking along. I couldn't do a thing. Its jaws clamped on the single shoulder strap of this sarong and lifted me right into the air. Thank heaven it didn't bite any lower or it would have cut my shoulder to the bone."

"Birds? Here?" Dawlish looked mystified.

"Certainly," Captain Bronson told him. "I've seen 'em—but I wouldn't call 'em birds. Sort of round things with big bellies which move at a terrific speed."

"That's right," Bernice agreed eagerly; then her expression changed. "Oh, I—er— Excuse me! I don't seem to know you."

"Captain Bronson—Miss Forbes." Dawlish introduced, and to the girl he added a brief explanation; then he came back to the point at issue. "A bird, eh? Can you describe it?"

"From a height it looked round, nearly like a disc, but when it came lower it opened its wings and beak. I'd call it a sort of flying tortoise, of tremendous size. When it is in the air it draws its head and wings into its outer casing and just hurtles through space. Don't ask me how. I was carried along at dizzying speed for what seemed dozens of miles, and I was at least three hundred feet from the ground. The thing's head wasn't fully retracted because of holding me, but its wings were."

"And what happened finally?" Dawlish asked.

"It settled in a colony amongst thousands of others of the horrible things. A whole plateau of them there

seemed to be. That was not all, either." The look of horror came back into Bernice's eyes. "There were dozens of skeletons, human ones! I don't know what ghastly sort of carnage had gone on there at some time in the past, but the remains were certainly in evidence. The only answer can be that the birds are carnivorous. There was I, in the midst of them, lying on the ground, and feeling sure I was going to be eaten up or something."

"Obviously you weren't," Lucy said, looking most unconvinced. "So what happened?"

"A storm saved me. I'm sure those vile things were going to tear me to pieces, but just then a terrific wind got up. Thunder, lightning, and it rained in a deluge. Every one of those birds took to the air and left me alone. I gathered they were afraid of the elements, and I know I was. But my fear of them returning was much greater so I got on the move and ran, and ran—and ran. I was in the storm all the time it raged. Sometimes I had to crawl on my hands and knees to avoid being blown over by the wind, and I'm sure it was only a miracle that saved me being struck by lightning. I seemed to go over endless miles of fields. I just kept going."

"Then?" Dawlish prompted.

"More by luck than anything else, after I'd been wandering for ages, I caught a glimpse of the distant woodland and knew that was where I had to head for to find you. I did just that—and came back."

"Which would seem to prove," Nick said finally, "that this place isn't so untenanted by life as we thought."

"No reason why it shouldn't have life," Dawlish answered. "We know there are fish, so birds are not uncommon in such a set-up. I doubt human life, though, of our type. After all, if a perfect stranger landed on a South Sea island in the normal world he might be prepared to swear that there was no life anywhere. Regarding these flying tortoises, how many times have you seen them, Captain?"

"Dozens of times! Once the infernal things made an attack on my ship but I drove 'em off. I blasted one of 'em to bits with gunfire, and they never came again. They're dangerous."

"Where do you suppose they got the humans whose bones Bernice saw?" Betty asked, horrified.

"From our own normal world perhaps," Dawlish replied slowly. "Don't you begin to see a significance about these birds?"

"The only thing I can see," Lucy replied, "is that our hopes of walking back home, as we thought Berny had done, have been blown sky high. We're further off than ever."

"The point I am making." Dawlish said patiently, "is that the flying tortoises with their retracted head and wings—which perhaps fly by some kind of natural jet propulsion through their bodies—might very closely resemble the vaunted 'flying saucers' seen in various parts of our own plane."

"Why, of course!" Bernice exclaimed. "At a great height that's just what they'd look like."

"By the Great Reef, what's a flying saucer?" Bronson

demanded. "Believe me, there have been times when I've thought myself going over the border of sanity, but I've always been level-headed compared to you people! You talk in riddles and for the most part don't seem to have the vaguest idea what you're doing."

"We haven't," Nick sighed. "That's just the trouble."

"Flying saucers are mysterious flying objects seen from time to time in our own plane," Dawlish explained. "They've been variously described as visitors from another planet to a figment of indigestion. Nobody really knows—but it begins to look as if we might! Since a three-dimensioned person has no difficulty in moving in one or two dimensions, then a four-dimensioned creature would have no difficulty in moving in three. It could quite easily cross into our plane at any time it wished—and probably does if flying saucers are what they now seem to be."

"Then you think," Nick asked slowly, "that maybe people who have vanished from our plane have been snatched away by these flying tortoise saucers, or whatever they are?"

"Possible, isn't it? Not in every case, of course, such as disappearances by people in busy streets and surrounded in some cases by witnesses. Those have been genuine sidesteps into the fourth dimension—just as in the case of ships, airplanes, and so forth. But I'd certainly like to wager that many disappearances of humans can be traced to these things."

"Only one thing against that theory," Harley said, musing. "Flying saucers have only been heard of in

the past few years. What about disappearances prior to that?"

"Flying saucers," Dawlish replied, "have been heard of for many, many years, Mr. Brand. Records go back into the last century. It is only recently that flying saucers have become really noticeable, which I attribute to them being in greater numbers than ever before."

"And if they come here?" Lucy questioned. "Can we fight them? How about it, Berny?"

"It'd be safer to run for it," she answered. "To the ship there, for instance. They're too big to fight without guns. Of course, since they have never flown down here except for the odd one that attacked me—we'll probably not be molested. But I think we ought to be prepared."

"I wonder," Dawlish said, after a moment, "if perhaps these birds might be useful to us. If they can fly into our own plane and bring back human beings—which seems a reasonable theory—then why can't they take human beings back there?"

"Sounds too risky!" Nick shook his head.

"Of course it's risky," Dawlish agreed. "But surely we are all agreed that any risk is better than stopping here?"

"Sweet oil of Judah, you don't expect to ride one of those blasted birds piggy-back, do you?"

"If necessary, Captain. I'm willing to ride Pegasus any time!"

"And suppose," Bernice asked, "that in flying from

one plane to the other we get torn to bits, or something?"

"Why should we? We came here without hurt." Then before anybody could comment further Dawlish added, "The problem is how to get one of these birds without getting mixed up with a whole flock of them—"

"Simple, simple," Bronson broke in quickly. "Use fish. It's the only food, apart from a little green stuff, that the infernal birds have to eat in this plane. It was only when I left some fish on the deck one morning, intending to do some gutting later, that I was attacked by the birds. They can scent fish miles away."

"That's it!" Dawlish snapped his fingers. "We'll get some fish immediately—"

"If it will bring one bird it will bring flocks of them," Harley pointed out. "Better be prepared for that, but as far as I can see we've no weapons."

"I've one rifle and large supplies of ammunition," Bronson said, "so maybe I'd better go and get it— No, can't do that," he broke off. "I'd need all of you, once again. Maybe this will help instead?"

He felt under the rear of his thick reefer jacket and produced a heavy revolver.

"Fully loaded," he explained. "I carry it around in case of emergency."

"That should help," Dawlish agreed, and stepped over to examine it. Nick made it his opportunity to settle down at Bernice's side.

"Glad you're back, Berny," he murmured. "I missed you."

"Sure?" She gave him a suspicious glance.

"Honest! You went off in a huff because I raised objections about our getting married—then when I found you'd vanished, and probably back to our own plane, I could have kicked myself."

Bernice smiled faintly. "I don't think we'll ever get back, Nick—honest! So surely, if we are to finish our lives here, we can do it as we intended to do it and become husband and wife?"

"Yes, I think we should," Nick agreed finally. "And we have a legally qualified person now who can perform the ceremony." Nick nodded towards Bronson who had now gone to the water's edge and was apparently looking for fish.

"Queer old duck," Bernice murmured, studying him. "I get the idea he's a bit—well, you know!"

"Wouldn't you be after twenty years alone in this plane?" Nick held down a hand as he got to his feet and assisted Bernice to rise.

"You mean we get married now?" she asked.

"No reason why not. Hey, Captain Bronson!" Nick called. Bronson turned and came over, watched by Dawlish, Harley, his wife, and Betty.

"Can you marry us?" Nick asked, nodding towards Bernice.

"I can, but why the devil should I?"

"Well—er—to legalize the life which Miss Forbes and I wish to live together. Dawlish could do it as the leader of the party, only it wouldn't be strictly ethical. You, as a sea captain, have the authority."

"Maybe I have, but I'm not using it. Great mizzen masts, think what you're doing! Isn't it terrible enough that you are stuck in this ghastly land like the rest of us without plotting to probably bring others into it? And I'm talking about children!" Bronson yelled, his beard projecting. "What kind of a life would it be for them?"

"Well, we—"

"No!" Bronson snapped. "And don't bother me!"

He turned his back deliberately and looked out to sea.

Nick scratched the back of his neck and then gave Dawlish an anxious glance. Dawlish was as unperturbed as ever—lean, dark brown with unseen ultraviolet radiation, a faint smile on his lips.

"Have to let you do it, Dawlish," Nick said.

"Sorry, sir. I don't feel justified whilst there is a legally qualified person, namely Captain Bronson."

"Dammit, man, you heard what he just said!"

"Yes, sir—and quite candidly I agree with him." Nick stared blankly for a moment, and for that matter so did the rest of the party. Betty, indeed, was looking more astonished than anybody.

"Agree with him?" she repeated. "What on earth do you mean?"

Dawlish looked about him. Bronson had also come up to listen.

"Perhaps," Dawlish said, "I should make the situation clear as far as I am concerned. You must be aware by now that Miss Danvers—Betty—and I—are—"

"You don't usually stumble around like this,

Dawlish," Harley commented bluntly. "What's the matter with you?"

"Oh, give him a chance!" Lucy objected. "It's an awkward subject."

"Not awkward—delicate," Dawlish corrected. "Betty and I are very much in love with each other— yet I have sidestepped Betty's request that we should marry, and I think that she—and all of you—should know why."

"Not if it's private," Nick said hastily.

"I think," Dawlish continued, "that we're all too infernally selfish, and I include myself. We see only our own earthly desires and give no heed to the consequences. Captain Bronson hit the nail dead on the head when he said what he did about children. What would it be like for them?"

There was a silence and exchange of glances.

"As natural men and women we know that we desire, but wouldn't it be kinder to possible progeny if we went no further? This plane we are in is the worst form of solitary confinement ever devised. It gives us health, yes, because the air is pure; but it also does something equally peculiar. It gives us an almost endless life. Endless life to endure in a world where nothing ever happens! Nature in her most ironical mood never devised anything more brilliant. And there is something else."

"Could there be?" Nick asked irritably.

"Any progeny might remain eternal infants," Dawlish finished. "Born, yes, but never evolving, or if

they did so at all it would be at such a slow pace that it would be imperceptible. I don't have to tell you again that Time here virtually stands still compared to our normal conception of it."

"Well, since that's how it is," Nick said, "I suppose you and I, Berny, will remain very good friends—or else disgrace this august company at some time by being unable to believe in Dawlish's ethics! Come down from your pedestal, Dawlish," he implored. "We're stuck here and each of us has the right to say what he or she is going to do."

"Right!" Bernice agreed flatly.

"Makes no difference to me," Hatley commented, with a dry grin. "Lucy and I were married long ago."

"Of which I hardly need reminding," Lucy murmured. "It took a place like this, though, to make us come together. I'm even starting to see points in you, Harley, which I rather like. I never had the time in the ordinary way. You're bad-tempered, edgy, and blunder in where most folks would hesitate, but I think you have a sterling ring somewhere."

"Can't have," he shrugged. "I've been singled out as the most selfish man in the party. Oh well, if others wish to behave like penitents it's no business of mine. I'm going for a walk."

"And I'll come with you," Lucy decided. "I'd like to know you even better, Mr. Brand." They turned and went up the beach together, leaving Nick and Bernice, and Dawlish and Betty staring after them almost in envy.

"Know something?" Nick asked. "I do believe those two are going to finish up as the only happy pair in the party, and they started out by being the most miserable." He stood thinking for a moment, his face becoming grimmer. "Was there ever such a set-up?" he demanded at last. "The everlasting silence, a sun you can't see, a girl you can't have, things you mustn't do, and age you can't attain—an eternal life like this will be purgatory!"

He swung away, too morose to say anything more. Bernice followed him, catching up after a few moments. She caught at his arm.

"Nick, take it easy. For my sake."

"Easy! Great heavens!"

"This isn't like you, Nick. Usually you laugh your way through. 'Playboy' Clayton—"

"Playboy be hanged!" he nearly snarled. "I've grinned up to now because it seemed to be the only thing I could do, and I even did think the whole thing funny at times. But not any more. I realize now just what it means to be stuck here forever. Doomed and damned!"

Bernice gripped him again as he turned to move on.

"Last time, Nick, I was the one who flew off the handle when the matter of our getting married came up. Now it's you— Maybe Dawlish and the Captain are right. As time goes by we—"

"You should have married me whilst Dawlish was in the mood last time!" Nick snapped. "The Captain's put him off his stroke and he's turned into a reformer!"

Bernice lowered her hand and a glint came in her eyes.

"I would remind you, Nick, that it was you who wouldn't agree to marry me! You raked up some kind of story about explaining ourselves if we got home—"

"Oh, let me alone! I've had enough!"

Nick swung away, hands plunged in the pockets of his torn and dirty evening trousers. Bernice did not follow him. Instead she looked at the expanse of ocean, then at the scratches and bloodstains on her limbs. She did not move immediately.

For a time she gazed after Nick's receding figure; then she glanced towards the other members of the party some distance away. Bronson and Dawlish were at the water's edge, catching fish. Betty was standing watching them, looking like a child on holiday with her hands locked behind her and her head on one side.

Bernice sighed and once more surveyed the mirror-like ocean, then up towards a sun she could not see but whose rays were beating into her skin. She started walking into the sea.

CHAPTER SIX
THE THIRTY-FIRST OF JUNE

It was an hour later when Nick returned, still in a bad temper. He settled down amidst the other members of the party and for a while did not speak—then something seemed to occur to him.

"Say, Dawlish, where's Berny?" he asked.

"I don't know, sir. I thought she was with you."

"Not a bit of it. We squabbled and I went off on my own. All of which I blame on you, Dawlish, with your shortsighted ideas!"

"I spoke from the heart, sir, believe me."

"Great doldrums, what's that?" Bronson demanded, pointing. "I've been watching it, and it certainly isn't a fish."

The object he was indicating was being rocked back and forth by the receding tide and was half buried in the wet sand. It was partly yellow, partly brown, and it had the outlines of—

"Berny!" Nick shouted in horror, then he jumped up and raced away at top speed, reached the limp form in the yellow cut-down evening dress, and heaved at it desperately. Bernice's body came away from the sand

with a squelching noise, but even as he hauled Nick knew the worst. Picking the girl up he carried her to drier regions and laid her down. Bronson, Dawlish, and Betty came speeding up.

"She's—dead!" Betty gasped, her hand to her mouth.

"Yes." Nick's face was bitter as he glanced up. "Dead! Drowned! Whether by accident or design we don't know, but it certainly wouldn't have happened if one of you had kept an eye on her."

"The tragedy's horrible enough, sir, without looking for a scapegoat!" Dawlish retorted. "I didn't even know Miss Forbes had gone into the sea. Did you?" and he glanced at Bronson and Betty as they shook their heads.

"Maybe I caused it...." Nick was still on his knees, trying hard to keep tears out of his eyes. "Berny was the sort of girl to throw everything overboard if she saw no way out of a difficulty. Perhaps she couldn't see one out of this maze. I'd blown up in her face for some damned trivial reason, and she knew we were not going to marry— Maybe she thought it wasn't worth going on living in this solitude."

"Maybe lots of things," Betty said. "We'll certainly never know now. Only thing we can do is bury her."

Nobody said anything. Even in death Bernice still looked youthful and vigorous.

"She's the first," Bronson whispered, his eyes glinting. "There's got to be an end to all this some-where. I'd have done just what she's done twenty years ago, only I clung to the thought that I'd get back home.

Now I've been told by an expert that I never shall. This girl was sensible. She didn't wait mooning around until the utter insanity of everything turned her crazy, too—she finished it! Good girl!"

"Get a tarpaulin, Dawlish," Nick said tonelessly, getting to his feet.

"Tarpaulin, sir?"

"Yes, damn you! You don't suppose we're going to push her down in the sand as she is, do you? Hurry up!"

Dawlish went back to where the ship's tarpaulins were lying, for use as ground sheets, and came back with one of them. Bronson stood watching the two men and Betty reverently rolling the body in the sheet.

The most harrowing job of all for the trio was to scoop out the grave in the sand—but it had to be done as long as civilized notions remained in their minds. Into the hollow they finally lowered the body, then Dawlish turned to Nick.

"Do you wish me to perform the burial service, sir, or Captain Bronson?"

"You! I don't want that lunatic anywhere near me. But for him flavoring your mind with idiotic ideas Berny wouldn't be where she is now. Instead we'd have been married. Get the Bible."

Dawlish went, his lips tight. He returned after a while, performed the brief rite over the grave, and then helped to fill it in. By the time a rough cross of ship's timber had been erected, Harley and Lucy came back into view. They were arm-in-arm and actually

laughing with each other.

"Hello there!" Harley called, from the higher ground atop the beach. "I think you're right about the air here, Dawlish. It does do something to you. For about the first time in our married life Lucy and I actually understand one another! We were—what's this?"

Harley came to a stop and stared blankly at the grave, then to the three grim faces. Lucy frowned.

"Bernice," Nick explained, his voice flat and hard.

"Bernice?" Harley blinked. "But you can't mean she's—"

"I mean she's dead!" Nick cut in savagely. "Isn't that enough? What's the use of saying what her reasons were? Maybe she committed suicide; maybe she was accidentally drowned whilst bathing. We'll never know the truth. The first one of us to go. It's an omen, I tell you! One by one we'll all go!"

"Easy, sir," Dawlish muttered, gripping Nick's arm. "It's only natural for you to be overwrought, but—"

"Oh, shut up!" Nick blazed. "Can't you see what this place is doing to us? We're changing! Some of us are becoming much happier; others are becoming more morose. Your nature and mine, Harley, have changed places."

"Eh?" Harley asked in surprise, looking, fixedly at the grave.

"You're as light-hearted now as I was earlier on. I'm as bad-tempered as you used to be. Change our names, and except for our appearance being different, nobody would be any the wiser."

"Aren't things crazy enough without an idea like that?" Betty objected. "What about me? I haven't borrowed anybody else's temperament. I'm still Betty Danvers, and I still think we'll get out—one day!"

"Where's Captain Bronson?" Nick asked suddenly.

Dawlish glanced around. "No idea, sir. Strolled off on his own, I suppose—"

"Look here," Harley interrupted dogmatically, "I don't see why the subject Nick brought up should be dropped. Can individual natures change places? Has he become me, and have I become him?"

"Of course not, sir." Dawlish gave a serious smile. "Every living thing is an individual to itself, even in the fourth dimension. It is just coincidence that your nature has become more like Mr. Clayton's and his more like yours—as it used to be. Just the same, there is a reason for it."

"There is?" Lucy's eyebrows rose.

"In our own plane," Dawlish continued, "human beings and animals—for that matter every living thing—are affected by climatic changes. At least they are called that: actually they are depressional and exhilarational waves produced entirely by the free movement of electrons in the atmosphere which, in turn, affect the electrons making up living beings. We therefore have sudden crazes sweeping whole populaces; sudden crime waves without reason; sudden waves of deep melancholia which often result in anything from financial disaster to actual war. Then come the uplifting waves and we have an era of prosperity,

buoyant health, and so on. We believe such occurrences are in ourselves, but they are not. Scientists have proved that we just cannot help ourselves getting buoyant or depressed now and again. It is the power of electrons at work on us."

"And that's what is at work here?"

"Yes, but the effect here is much more intense because we are not physically suited to this dimension, therefore we feel the electronic changes with greater keenness. That, I am sure, is why Miss Forbes so suddenly took her own life without any real reason— for I'm sure none of us believes her death was just an accident."

"It might explain Captain Bronson's eccentricities, too," Lucy reflected. "Half the time he's sane and a good seaman; for the rest he's like something out of *Alice in Wonderland*."

"Exactly," Dawlish conceded. "It also explains your gradual transition from a happy-go-lucky temperament to one of gloomy foreboding, Mr. Clayton. It also explains, Betty, your absolute conviction that you haven't got heart trouble any more. In actual fact you probably still have your complaint, but your mind is so lightened of worry by electronic processes you refuse to believe it. Possibly, since the body always obeys the mind, you've unwittingly cured yourself. As for me—" Dawlish gave a shrug. "Well, I've felt changes, and analyzed them. I've chosen a middle course and tried to keep dead level. As leader, I feel that I must."

"And since these electronic changes must go on all

the time, how will we finish up?" Betty enquired.

"Dead!" snapped the voice of Captain Bronson from a few feet away. "That girl showed us, didn't she?"

The party turned to look at him. He had evidently approached in perfect silence in the sand; and now they came to notice it he had his big revolver in his hand.

"Yes, it's loaded," he said, interpreting the expressions. "But you don't think I'm going to waste bullets on you poor fools, do you? No. If I wasted any at all, it would be on you, Mr. Dawlish, for leading me up the garden path with your talk of escape."

"I fully believed, at the time, that I was right—"

"Shut up! That girl showed me today that there's only one way out of this prison, and I'm taking it—"

"Wait a minute!" Nick cried in alarm, leaping up—but he was too late: Bronson deliberately turned the gun upon himself and fired. Then he crumpled slowly into the sand, the weapon falling from his hand.

There was a stunned silence for a moment. Coming so quickly on top of Bernice's fate this second tragedy was a decided jolt.

Without speaking Nick went for a tarpaulin and within an hour a second grave was lying beside Bernice's. Those who remained looked at each other.

"Do you suppose," Betty asked at length, "that each one of us is going to do this sort of thing, finally?"

"I don't think Lucy or I will, anyhow," Harley said.

"No?" Dawlish looked questioningly—and Lucy too seemed a little surprised.

"I have a proposition, regarding my wife and

myself," Harley continued. "As you know, since we got stranded here we've come to know each other much better and, well, we'd rather like to behave as most married people do and have our own home, our own privacy, and everything."

"Oh?" Dawlish still looked puzzled.

"It's pretty certain, isn't it, that we're here for the rest of our lives?"

Dawlish shrugged. "You're as wise as I am, sir. I still hold out hope that perhaps we—"

"I'm afraid we don't—Lucy and I." Harley put an arm about her shoulders. "We talked it over during our walk, and we both came to the conclusion that we're almost glad things worked out the way they did. In the normal run of life we were getting terribly at logger-heads with each other, and most of it was my fault. I was making money so fast I'd no time for anything else. Now I know what a mistake it would have been had I lost Lucy."

"So you have a proposition?" Nick asked, anxious to get to the point.

Harley nodded and gave a faint smile. "Now Captain Bronson has finished things for himself, I can't see any reason why Lucy and I can't take over his home."

"Are you serious?" Betty asked, astonished. "You saw what the solitude did to Bronson. In time it would do the same to you."

"He was by himself," Harley pointed out. "In this case Luce and I will have each other. After all, since we have to stay here, we might as well do it in comfort

in a home already made."

"We had intended asking Captain Bronson if there was another ship we could turn into a home," Lucy put in. "As things have worked out, we didn't get the chance. We can easily take over his place and work out a new pattern for life."

"No worries, no money, no responsibilities." Harley's face broke into a smile. "Be a Paradise!"

"The decision is entirely for you to make, of course," Dawlish said, "but you have realized, I suppose, that once you get to the island of lost ships you'll stop there?"

"You'll come and visit us now and again, surely?" Lucy asked. "Not that we'll want to leave, but we'll certainly wish to know how you are getting on."

"We'll be all right," Dawlish replied. "We'll build another bungalow, or even take over this old tramp steamer as a home. For myself I want to remain around here and explore the possibilities of escape. How about you, Mr. Clayton?"

"I certainly prefer it to being on that lost ship island. And anyhow, two's company," he added.

"I go where Daw goes," Betty announced. "Always!"

"We'll go in the one remaining boat," Harley announced. "Perhaps you'll give a hand to get it released from the davits?"

So the job was done, and in the late evening, amidst the gray light of the cloudless, sunless sky, Harley and Lucy took their departure in the solitary open boat. Quite unafraid, they kept on waving, in between plying

the oars, until at last the deep mists of evening had enveloped them.

"That seems to be that," Nick said at length, drawing a deep breath. "Good luck to 'em. They'll certainly need—"

He paused, frowning at a curious drumming note distinctly noticeable in the twilight. With the seconds it changed to a dull droning: then suddenly there appeared out of the upper air three enormous shapes, hurtling straight for the beach.

"Birds!" Dawlish cried, whipping out the revolver he had taken from Bronson. "They've come after that fish we've laid out, just as Bronson said they would."

At the moment there were four of them, and it did not seem a particularly good idea to stand on the open beach and wait for something to happen. So, moving fast, Dawlish and Betty began to head towards the woodland, pausing in the gloom and looking back at Nick as he remained where he was.

"Come on, sir!" Dawlish yelled at him.

"Not me!" Nick called back. "I'd sooner take a madman's ride on a flying tortoise in the hope of getting back home, than stick around here and wait for something to happen."

"It's suicide!" Dawlish cried—then he whipped up his gun and fired at one of the enormous birds as it hurtled straight towards Nick. By a fraction it missed him as he ducked, and crashed down helplessly into the sand, there to flutter helplessly with its curious blunted wings. The remaining birds, startled by the report of

the gun, screeched upwards like living jet-planes and vanished in the mists.

"This is it!" Nick cried, running forward and sitting astride the shell-like back of the bird. "Couldn't be a better chance for me to ride Pegasus. When he recovers he'll carry me with him—either to some other part of this infernal wilderness or straight back home. I'm taking the risk."

"Do you realize what you're doing?" Dawlish shouted.

"Certainly I do. He can't attack me if I'm on top of him: his neck isn't long enough. I'm determined, Dawlish. I just don't care any more what happens? Understand?"

Dawlish hesitated, Betty hanging onto his arm. Both of them were about fifty yards from where Nick was now clinging to his weird steed; then before Dawlish could decide what to do the bird recovered sufficiently from its bullet wound to get on the move. Its wings projected firmly from the sides of its underbelly as it took to the air.

Nick, utterly desperate, had been prepared for wild flight, but he had never expected the terrific speed at which the weird bird moved. As Dawlish had long ago theorized, the bird flew by natural jet propulsion, sucking air through its queer entrails and ejecting it again with a screech from natural organs at the rear. It flew with dizzying velocity high over the beach, and then began wheeling.

Nick felt sick and horrified. He realized now what an

idiot he had been, but just at the moment he had taken the plunge he had been too tired of everything to care. Any chance, however outlandish, had seemed to offer more prospect than the much more remote one of a lucky accident. So he clung on, and the winged horror shot like a bullet through the gathering night. Nick felt the warm wind tearing past him and the wild dipping of the bird made his stomach feel as though it were turning inside out.

On and on the bird flew, leaving the beach infinitely far behind, climbing higher and higher into the crazy sky. Nick wondered if perhaps the monster were going to plunge between planes, and so back to the normal world—the one thing he hoped for.

But it did not happen. The bird had an intelligence he had never suspected. Knowing it could not dislodge its rider by ordinary methods, its only ambition seemed to be to free itself—and there was one sure way to do it. To go so high that eventually the air would be too cold and rarefied for Nick to hold on. This same air would be needed by the bird itself, of course, to propel its body but whether the human being would be able to retain a grip remained to be seen.

So it began to climb. Nick found the air growing cold. He began to shiver. He looked with eyes that were commencing to ache for some signs of a change in the face of things, some sign that he had perhaps crossed from one space to the other.

No such sign came. Only the rod-like stars above, blurred by the fantastic twisting of this crazy plane.

And down below a void, so far, so immeasurably deep, it might have been infinite space itself.

Nick began to yawn. He felt himself getting sleepy and he was breathing with difficulty. The bird had slowed down its ascent as the air thinned, but it was still going up. Up—ever up—and Nick stared dumbly into the emptiness. Then he felt his right hand slip on the shell back. His fingers had become numb. He tried to recover his grip, and failed—so he clung on with the remaining hand and that, too, slowly began to lose feeling.

"No!" Nick screamed helplessly, as he knew at last that the bird had deliberately risen to these heights for the sole purpose of destroying him. "No! *No*—!"

His remaining hand gave way and immediately his knees no longer had a grip on the smooth shell. He keeled sideways and dropped into the gulf. In the few brief seconds of anguish as he fell headlong into the infinite abyss he experienced a reaction of sudden happiness. He was going to join Bernice, going to escape this madman's world, going— Down, everlastingly down. Faster— Extinction!

And, from the beach, Betty and Dawlish had watched the bird's climb. Some curious internal discharge from it, perhaps on the principle of a glowworm, had made it visible as it climbed into the sky. It had risen like a thin rocket, ever up, until it had been lost amidst the sloping, crazy stars.

"He should have listened," Dawlish muttered, his arm going about Betty's shoulders. "Oh, the fool! The

fool! He'd never be able to stand those heights. What madness prompted him to attempt it? There never was a guarantee that the bird would fly into our own plane, anyway."

"The same madness which led Bernice and Bronson to commit suicide," Betty whispered. "The same madness which led Harley and Lucy to spend the rest of their lives on an island of lost ships.... All mad, in different ways. Madness need not always take a horrible form. Sometimes it is even pleasurable, as in the case of Lucy and Harley. You and I, Daw: perhaps we're mad, too. Those electronic processes you spoke of."

"Perhaps. It is not in a form which we can plainly distinguish as crazy—yet I suppose we are otherwise we would not be on this lonely beach nursing a dim illusion that we might get home—some day."

"It's gone!" Betty exclaimed suddenly, pointing into the sky.

Dawlish looked. "And that can only mean one thing. Poor Mr. Clayton!"

There was silence. They could assume Nick's fate, but instinctively, they knew they were right. Nick's gamble had failed and he had gone the same way as Bernice and Bronson.

"You realize," Betty said at last, "that you and I are alone in this fantastic place? That whatever is ahead of us we shall do together, until perhaps—"

"We'll make the ship our headquarters in case the birds come back," Dawlish said, stirring into activity

again. "And the first thing we must do is get a meal: it seems ages since we had one. By doing that we mean no disrespect to Mr. Clayton. I'm sure he would have agreed that the living must carry on."

"I wonder if they must," Betty mused. "Or is it perhaps the most sensible way to—end it all?" Dawlish lowered his arm from the girl's shoulders. Instead he took her arms and shook her gently.

"You are being influenced as they were," he said deliberately. "There's only one way to fight it. Ignore it! Defy it! I've felt the same many a time before, but I quenched it. It's an ever-present evil in this plane: a tremendous mental depression caused by the unaccustomed electronic waves. We have got to beat that influence, Betty, or go under for all time."

She made a sudden effort. "I'm all right now," she said. "It was just a thought, but now you've explained why it came to me, I'll be on the watch. Let's get to the ship."

They moved along the dark beach towards the vessel, gained the deck, and then went down the companionway to the captain's cabin. Dawlish lighted the oil lamps and then went out again to the storage-hold. By degrees he assembled a meal, adding to it a bottle of wine with cobwebs round its neck.

"Six of 'em stored away," he said, as Betty looked surprised. "Only thing I can find to drink."

"It isn't as though we've anything to celebrate," she said slowly.

"Depends on the point of view...." Dawlish uncorked

the bottle and poured the wine into two glasses; then he added, "Drink up—and when you've done that we'll have our meal."

"I still can't see what we have to celebrate."

"Well, at least we can touch glasses and hope for the best."

Betty settled down and the glasses clinked. She studied Dawlish's lean features as he drank the wine slowly.

"From the way you talk, Daw, it sounds as if you think there is something to celebrate," she said.

"It's more a personal than a general matter," he replied.

"Up to now I have had to set myself up as an example to the others and refrain from doing any of the things which I banned for them. Now it doesn't matter. There's only you and me. I am assuming that you still feel the same towards me as you did before?"

Betty smiled slightly. "If you mean do I still love you, well of course I do! I am—"

"I was against marriage," Dawlish broke in, thinking. "I agreed with Bronson that it would not be right. But nature has a tremendous compulsion, Betty, which I do not believe you or I are strong enough to resist. For my part I don't intend to anymore. For the sake of the civilized education we have had we must solemnize our marriage. We can do it on the Bible. It will not mean anything without witnesses, but at least our consciences will be clear. You agree?"

Betty did not answer. Instead she got up, hunted

around the cabin for a moment, then returned to the table with the Bible. She laid it down with a significant movement, and waited.

"You and I, and Mr. and Mrs. Brand, are probably the only human beings in this plane," Dawlish continued, a faraway look in his eyes. "Whether any children will come of the two unions we do not know, but if they do, let us pray to heaven that they will grow, and live, and not remain eternal infants."

Betty filled the wine glasses up again. As she sipped she put a thought into words.

"Something's bothering you, Daw. What is it? Believe me, I'm entirely with you in everything you say and do."

"Nothing much," he shrugged. "Just that, if we ever do get home again, we must legalize everything. Now, let's have our meal."

Betty settled down and began to eat—and she drank more wine. Dawlish drank too and despite the food, which had a steadying influence, they were neither of them particularly comfortable when at last they rose from the table. Had they not known the ship was beached and the tide fast receding they could have sworn it was on the move, so definitely did the cabin seem to sway.

"Damned powerful wine," Dawlish muttered, picking his words and hanging onto Betty's arm as she stumbled forward. "We ought to have remembered that. Been stored a long time, y'know."

"Uh-huh," Betty acknowledged, and reached the

cabin doorway by degrees.

On the way up the companion-ladder she slipped once or twice and Dawlish had to haul her back to the level again; then presently they came out into the open air, the night, and the rod-like stars. It should have cleared their buzzing heads a little, but it did not. They felt as if their knees were giving way and the deck was swirling horribly with every move they made.

"Soon be all right," Dawlish said, with far more hope than conviction.

They gained the rope ladder hanging over the ship's side and to descend it was a real work of art—even for Dawlish, who had a stronger control over his movements than Betty. She was quite unable to find the rungs and at last Dawlish had to carry her over his shoulder. Gaining the beach he put her on her feet again.

As usual there was the aching silence, except for the lap of the waves from the gentle, deserted ocean. Then, for a reason she could not explain Betty found herself weeping copiously.

"Okay, Betty, take it easy," Dawlish murmured, hugging her to him. "I know the outlook gets tougher the more we contemplate it, but we'll find a way to master ourselves somehow."

"I'm frightened," Betty panted. "More frightened tonight than I've ever been before. Maybe it's the wine. I wouldn't know. I feel so horribly shut away from all the things I've ever known. There's nothing but this awful, silent world, which we'll never understand. The empty ocean, the weird stars, the deadly birds, the— I

can't stand it much longer, Daw! Honestly I can't!"

"Take it easy," he insisted. "You're riding those electronic waves again, or else it's the reaction of that blasted wine. You're getting into just the mood of profound melancholia that led Miss Forbes and Bronson to kill themselves. It must not happen to you, Betty! It just mustn't!"

What she would have done had he released his grip upon her he did not know. He just didn't give her the chance, though at times he could feel her making ineffectual efforts to tug away towards the tide line.

"We'll take a walk," he said decisively. "It will help to clear the muddle of that confounded wine out of our heads. You will feel better then. Remember what I told you, my dear, you must master these onslaughts which are being made upon your mind. They'll always be present, so a resistance must be built up against them."

"And what about us?" Betty asked, as they began walking in the loose sand. "What happens now? Do we keep to the original idea of marrying and witnessing our own union?"

"No other way now. Maybe we can capture those ghostly voices again, then we shan't feel quite so shut out."

They left the beach and strolled through the midst of the dry, crackling grass. Neither of them were walking with any ease. The wine was twirling their heads round so they had little consciousness of what they were really doing, and in their knees was a desperate weakness.

"Is there any point in anything any more?" Betty asked at last, her voice low. "Just where is the sense in prolonging things?"

"Why will you not fight?" Dawlish demanded angrily, stopping and shaking her. "You promised you would, yet with every statement you make you're sinking lower! Much more of this and every spark of vitality will have gone out of you! Get a grip on yourself, Betty! Remember that you said some time ago you rather liked being here. It has improved your heart, for one thing—"

"Oh, I felt different then. Now there is only you and I left, I—I sort of want to lie down and fade away. A world in which nothing ever happens. I'm sure I'll never be able to face it, Daw, not even with you at my side. Everything seems so utterly—unnatural!"

"You'll face it, Betty, because I'll see that you do! Now come along. Fresh air's the only thing to straighten us out. And don't get the impression that I don't feel as depressed as you do. I do—but I'm straining every nerve and muscle to keep myself above it. We musn't go under. Betty. That way lies death."

Betty did not answer. Dawlish's arm was about her shoulders again, gently but firmly moving her. So she kept on walking, closing her eyes presently to shut out the irritating, ridiculous visions of rod-like stars and pearl-gray heavens.

"We're going a long way," she said at length, opening her eyes and looking about her. "I'm getting tired, or else my legs are weak."

Dawlish glanced back. "We've only come about half a mile as yet. I want to see if we can pick up those voices again. They may restore our flagging spirits...."

The grass continued to crackle under their feet. They had become so used to it they did not trouble to look down. Just as they had become accustomed to the rod-like stars, so they did not bother to glance up. Straight ahead: that was the only direction in which they gazed, and this only with difficulty with their vision so distorted by hangover from the wine.

But even a hangover could not account for hedges where none had been before, or the curious hardness that the ground had assumed. It still cracked, with a different note, and it cut sharply into bare feet.

Dawlish came to an abrupt stop, his ears measuring along drawn-out note that quivered into silence on the warm air.

"Betty." His voice was a husky whisper. "Betty, take a look!"

"Huh?" She opened her eyes sleepily and looked around her. At the dim hedges, the fields, and then the stars. They were misty with heat haze, but they were round points and not rod-like bars.

For several seconds there was a tremendous silence. Then from the far distance came the sounds of an approaching train. *A train*—?

"We're back!" Dawlish yelled, as the truth burst upon him. "Betty, we're back! The stars are normal. That was a train we heard a moment ago! We're walking on rough, stone-surfaced roadway where formerly it was

grass."

Betty was cold sober now as she still looked around her.

"I heard a sound," she said quickly, remembering. "Just like the queer gong we heard when we drove in here to begin with—I mean there. Wherever it is—" She was hopelessly confused, too delighted to speak, too frightened to say much in case it should prove a delusion.

"Look!" Dawlish gripped her arm and pointed. Dimly in the starlight they could see something white standing not far away. Regardless of cuts to their bare feet they raced along to it and it merged into a white signpost. It said—TO MYTHORN TOWERS.

"It's it! It's *it*!" Betty shouted, executing a war dance. "And there's the church behind it— But look at the time!"

The weather-stained gold fingers were just visible, pointing to two minutes past midnight. Dawlish looked about him, mystified, then he gazed at the dust in the lane which led to the distant major road—that road they should have reached and never had.

"See," he directed, pointing.

Though there was only the starlight it was reflected back brightly enough from the dust to reveal the tyre marks of a car—marks freshly made. They went a certain distance and then stopped dead. Beyond them the dust of the lane was undisturbed.

"Our car tracks?" Betty questioned at last, bewildered.

"No doubt of it."

"But, Daw, they can't be! Look at the time we have been away and the things we have done."

"I know; but look at the number of things you can do in a dream and it only lasts a split second in actual fact. Some thinkers aver that dreams are excursions into the fourth dimension: if so, the time-factor is thereby verified."

"I just don't understand."

"Perhaps we never shall. The fact remains that these freshly-made tracks do belong to the car I was driving. I have good reason to recognize that particular tread. And that gong note we heard as we stepped back was the rear half of the last stroke of twelve from the church tower there. Remember how we heard it cut off as we crossed over?"

"Yes. Yes, of course I do." Betty was still looking about her. "But it's still impossible! It means we haven't been away any time at all!"

"Maybe we haven't! Remember those voices? They were speaking before midnight. We drove into nowhere at almost the last stroke of twelve, and came out again as the last stroke was still striking. In the interval—if any—we lived at ultrafast speed contrary to normal time. And the funniest thing of the lot is that we got out when we were more or less tight! Which is probably why we did it. In not looking for a way out we found it."

"Well," Betty said, commencing to assimilate things at last, "the best thing we can do is go straight to

Mythorn Towers and tell them everything."

"No," Dawlish broke in quietly. "It wouldn't do. Betty. Not a soul would believe us. We might even get ourselves certified! Look at us! Nearly naked, and brown as Polynesians. The folks at Mythorn Towers would think it was some kind of fancy dress charade. We don't want to spend the rest of our lives in a booby-hatch, do we?"

"No," Betty muttered. "Of course not. Which makes the situation decidedly difficult. There's going to be an awful lot of questioning soon. What has happened to Nick and Berny, for one thing. Where are Lucy and Harley Brand? How do we even begin to answer?"

"We don't. We might put ourselves right in line for a murder charge or something. Our only chance now is to disappear quickly to somewhere quiet and start life all over again under different names. You without your father's millions, and me without a job. It can be done—if you're willing."

"I'm willing—but how do we do it? We've no money, and no clothes that can be called decent. We wouldn't get above a mile

"In my home I have some savings in cash," Dawlish replied. "I have a small cottage about twenty miles from here. My mother was born and died there, and of course I stopped living there when I went into service with Mr. Clayton. But I kept it on for my time off. If we walk most of the night we can reach the cottage by dawn. There are some clothes there too. Some of my mother's that she left behind might fit you. Then we'll

get away as quietly as possible, maybe to the Continent, before any questions are asked."

"Which means we'll be fugitives for the rest of our lives! Have you thought of that?"

"Yes. Fugitives from an asylum. That is what we have to avoid at all costs. One cannot have an adventure like we did and expect to be believed, Betty. The human mind just wouldn't take it in, any more than we could ourselves at the beginning. The penalty for our experience, if we wish to remain free, is that we have to forget everything we ever did, and everybody we ever knew. There will just be—ourselves."

"And we'll get married?" Betty straightened up. "All right; that's good enough for me. The only person likely to mourn me is my father—and he was getting pretty tired of my draining on his bank account, too. In any case, he was under the impression I'd only six months to live, so if I disappear sooner it won't be much of a shock. And you haven't anybody who cares?"

"Only you."

Betty started moving slowly, picking her way uncomfortably in her bare feet on the pebbly ground. Dawlish moved to her side, and then they both stopped as a light suddenly flashed upon them. They could see a solid form behind it.

"Now, now, what's all this about?" asked a heavy voice. "It isn't all that hot tonight, is it?"

Dawlish smiled. "That's all right, constable. We're not doing any harm."

"I should hope not." P.C. Andrews of the Little

Brook constabulary sounded dubious. "Just the same it's against the law to be indecently clad on a public highway, even at night. Now, according to the regulations, it's my duty to see that you—"

"I don't think you will, constable," Betty murmured, turning on her sweetest smile. "You see, the explanation is that we're in a South Sea island play at Mythorn Towers. Henry T. is putting it on for the benefit of his guests at the house warming. We managed to escape for a while so we could be together. We never gave a thought to our dress."

"Mmmm." P.C. Andrews switched off his flashlight and cleared his throat. "All right, if that's the case. But get back to Mythorn Towers quickly."

"We will," Dawlish promised. "Come on, Betty."

Glad to make their escape they went up the lane, but the moment they were out of sight of Andrews they went in the opposite direction to Mythorn Towers.

"He's going to remember us later when the story of our disappearance travels far and wide," Betty remarked.

"And how much credence will he get? He saw two deeply sun-burned people in the flimsiest attire. Hardly sounds like the staid chauffeur Dawlish and Betty Danvers dying of heart disease, does it?"

"I'm not dying now, Daw," Betty murmured. "I never felt better in my life. Whatever else that plane did, it certainly cured me, and one day I'll have a doctor verify it."

Six months later she did just this, in Paris, and

nothing whatever could be found wrong with her. During this six months the mysterious disappearance of millionaire Nick Clayton and his friends had hit the headlines and his lawyers had done everything in their power, with the help of Scotland Yard and innumerable advertisements, to trace Nick's whereabouts. But of course they had drawn a complete blank.

So, slowly, the mystery faded out, and on the outskirts of Paris Dawlish and Betty were a perfectly happy married couple. To themselves they kept the secret of the weird adventure through which they had passed.

Rarely indeed did they even mention it, busy making their new life together—but when the warm summer evenings came, they used to walk in the glow of the twilight and could not help but think again of that strange land with its elongated stars, its island of lost ships, its sudden violent tempests, its otherwise perpetual calmness. Land without shadows, without sun, without moon. Land without hope, and yet—no, not without hope. Harley and Lucy Brand had elected to stay in the weird plane for all time, so with them at least hope could not have been dead.

"What I still cannot fathom is when it happened," Betty declared one evening, as she and her husband returned slowly home. "Everything is so normal again now. You making good money, our own little home, and maybe a child soon. Yet there is always the feeling, to me, that we lost a chunk out of our lives somewhere, although the calendar and the clock say we never lost

a second! That suggests that we added something, yet I don't know where it came in or if it even happened at all."

"It happened, dearest, and it was added to our normal span of life." Dawlish was as quiet and incisive as ever. "As for when it happened—well, we can only add a date of our own. One that does not exist. Let's say it all happened on the Thirty-First of June."

Betty smiled. The non-existent date fitted the situation exactly. She clung more tightly to Dawlish as they walked along in the soft dusk.

"That's it!" she murmured. "We are the only human beings who ever stepped out of this world and came back again—and yet lived many days and nights in the space of no time at all. We lived it all on the Thirty-First of June."

ABOUT THE AUTHOR

British writer **JOHN RUSSELL FEARN** was born near Manchester, England, in 1908. As a child he devoured the science fiction of Wells and Verne, and was a voracious reader of the Boys' Story Papers. He was also fascinated by the cinema, and first broke into print in 1931 with a series of articles in *Film Weekly*.

He then quickly sold his first novel, *The Intelligence Gigantic*, to the American magazine, *Amazing Stories*. Over the next fifteen years, writing under several pseudonyms, Fearn became one of the most prolific contributors to all of the leading US science fiction pulps, including such legendary publications as *Astounding Stories*, *Startling Stories*, *Thrilling Wonder Stories*, and *Weird Tales*.

During the late 1940s he diversified into writing novels for the UK market, and also created his famous superwoman character, The Golden Amazon, for the prestigious Canadian magazine, the Toronto *Star Weekly*. In the early 1950s in the UK, his fifty-two novels as "Vargo Statten" were bestsellers, most notably his novelization of the film, *Creature from the Black Lagoon*.

Apart from science fiction, he had equal success with westerns, romances, and detective fiction, writing an amazing total of 180 novels—most of them in a period of just ten years—before his early death in 1960. His work has been translated into nine languages, and continues to be reprinted and read worldwide.